Lagoonfire

Lagoonfire

Francesca Forrest

AnnorlundaBooks

Cover design by Susan Lavoie.

Published in the United States by Annorlunda Books.

Queries: info@annorlundaenterprises.com

First Edition

ISBN-13: 978-1-944354-55-8

I was on my way to visit the retired gods of Sweet Harbor District when I received a communication from Decommissioner Five, my superior at the Ministry of Divinities. *Large seawater incursion at Daybreak Ventures development site: potential engineering failures dismissed, ditto active deities. Please confirm it's not Laloran-morna.*

I don't think it's my own sensitivities that made me sense frustration in the message. I'm not the Ministry's favorite decommissioner of deities, to put it mildly. It's not that I'm bad at my job. I have a fine work ethic—Five acknowledges that—and above-average performance. It's just that for some reason my assignments often end up being complicated cases, and when a case is complicated, the solution may be unorthodox. The Ministry hates unorthodox solutions.

And all right: I'll admit that Laloran-morna's decommissioning wasn't my most stellar performance. I should have petitioned to decline the assignment. Laloran-morna—the god of the warm ocean waves of the rainy season—was the last of the Sweet Harbor gods. When my grandparents were children, they had worshiped those gods—the last generation to do so. I grew up with stories of the Sweet Harbor gods' exploits and rivalries: in a sense I grew up with Laloran-morna. That connection made my heart soar when the job came to me, but it's exactly why I ought to have turned it down. It's hard to decommission gods you have a relationship with, even an indirect one. But it was my first year in the field, I was overconfident, and the results, well... It turned out to be easier to divest Laloran-morna of his divinity than of the sea. The old man who remained when the decommissioning was complete had salt in his eyebrows and thin streams of water trickling down his spine and legs, and the odor of the ocean clinging to him. The dripping-wetness went away after a day or two, but even now, eleven years later, seawater finds its way to him when he's distressed. Shopkeepers hesitate to welcome him in, and drivers of courtesy vehicles have been known to ignore his attempts to flag them down—which ensures an inconvenient tidal pool or waterspout at the curb where he's left standing.

So I could understand why the Ministry suspected Laloran-morna might have something to do with Daybreak Ventures' flooding. The consortium plans a luxury hotel, a high-end shopping district, and a rainforest park for land reclaimed from what once was the northern edge of Lotus Estuary—waters the Sweet Harbor gods and their worshipers wrangled and fought over in legend and history. Diverting a river, filling in an estuary, and then building on it? You can see how that might offend a retired Sweet Harbor god. But none of the gods had mentioned it to me even in passing, and I visit them once a week.

But with Five's communication logged on my unicom, I was going to have ask some questions—first to the remaining retired Sweet Harbor gods who were up and about, and then to Laloran-morna himself. He *wasn't* up and about. To be blunt, he was dying. People don't like to think about it, but as soon as deities are decommissioned, they enter into mortality, which means eventually they die.

Honestly, I couldn't believe he'd be spending his energies fuming about a development project, even one where Lotus Estuary used to be. But I'd see what the others thought and take it from there.

The other Sweet Harbor gods were in the long, narrow park behind Promise of Unity Primary School and its associated childcare center, at one of the park's concrete tables for games of tiles. Mr. Tamlo, the canniest of all the juice vendors in this area, had pulled his cart alongside the tables. The cart has a sunshade made from real palm leaves—like the thatch that was common for houses centuries ago. It makes the retired gods nostalgic, and Mr. Tamlo knows it. He also knows their favorite juices— mangosteen for Malirin, pomalo-and-lime for Anin, exotic strawberry for Nakona, guava for Kadiuk. Laloran-morna, I recalled, always had passionfruit. Judging from the collection of discarded cups in Mr. Tamlo's trash bag, the gods had been there a while. And it was hot—only a little past midday. There was a bit of a breeze, but even so, the air felt close and steamy, like exhalations from a dragon.

"Sweeting!" exclaimed Nakona, calling me by the nickname my grandparents gave me. At work, I'm known by my decommissioner number—I'm Decomissioner Thirty-Seven—but with the retired Sweet Harbor gods, I'm Sweeting. When they call me that, it makes me feel like I'm part of a family in a way I never do, otherwise—not since my grandparents passed away.

Nakona's the only woman in the group. She was a goddess of tides; now she's a stocky matron who pulls her iron-grey hair back with a tortoiseshell clasp and wears black sunglasses to protect her pale blue sea-glass eyes—so startling in her deep brown face. Kadiuk was decommissioned longest ago—back when I was still a child. Other Sweet Harbor gods who were decommissioned after Kadiuk have passed away, but Kaduik carries on, more bent over, fewer and fewer hairs clinging to the sides of his shiny bald head, but eyes as sharp and bright as ever.

After we'd all exchanged hugs, Nakona ordered Mr. Tamlo to fix me a strawberry juice, prompting the others to order me their favorite drinks, whereupon I suggested the compromise I always suggest—a mix of all the juices. The gods always look horrified, and Mr. Tamlo always gives me whatever's most plentiful. Today that was mango.

"Who's winning?" I asked, looking at the scattering of tiles on the table. They don't play with ordinary tiles; theirs are painted with shallow-draft boats and outriggers, boats with crab-claw sails and tilted sails, and warriors armed with spine-tipped spears, powerful bows, and blowpipes. They play out the battles they and their followers fought, but the rules of the game mean, as Anin grumbled, that the outcomes aren't historically accurate.

"You're just a sore loser," Nakona said, smiling like a well-fed cat, which answered my initial question.

"If Lolo were here, things would be different." Anin sighed. "Lolo" was what the others called Laloran-morna. Anin had been the god of storms, storms that swelled Laloran-morna's warm waves during the rainy season. The two of them fit together like two halves of a clam shell. Since Laloran-morna's decline, Anin has grown morose.

"You have to learn to stand on your own," said Malirin, patting Anin's hand. Of course Malirin would say that: as god of the cool breezes that blow down from the continent during the dry season, he had been more a divinity of the land than the sea, aloof from the others.

"Speaking of Lolo," I said, "I'm going to call on him next, and I was wondering if there's anything I should know — any changes in his condition, or mood, or...?"

"We should have insisted on bringing him out this morning," said Anin, looking away abruptly and blinking rapidly.

"We have to trust the medics," Nakona replied. "They know how these mortal bodies work." She raised her arms, as if for inspection, then let them drop. To me she said, "They told us the air quality was too poor," and then to Anin, "You wouldn't want to bring him out and have him collapse."

Anin didn't reply.

"But he hasn't said anything about anything particular bothering him—nothing new, I mean?" I pressed.

The retired gods exchanged glances.

"Is it—" Nakona began.

"Lagoonfire season," Anin said, nodding.

They had lost me.

"Lagoonfire," Anin repeated. "Back in our day, the lagoons and estuaries used to glow with it at this time of year. Put your hand in it, walk through it, you'll glow too. Glow, but not burn."

"Oh! Some kind of bioluminescence," I said.

"Lolo always steals away for a day or two during lagoonfire season—private business," Nakona said. "You never noticed?"

I shook my head mutely. I was imagining lagoonfire. I'd never seen it, and with all the land reclamation going on, I wondered if I ever would. The sun glinting on my unicorn brought me back to my task.

"So you don't think he's angry over, for instance, the Daybreak Ventures development?" I asked.

The former deities looked at me blankly a moment.

"Oh—she means all that work going on where Lotus Estuary used to be," said Malirin.

"I'll never understand why the recent generations love land so much more than sea," muttered Kadiuk.

"Daybreak Ventures," Nakona repeated. Then her face broke into a smile. "I've heard about that development—there's going to be a rainforest park with a maglift train running through it. I want to ride that when it's done."

Kadiuk snorted and Malirin rolled his eyes.

"Lolo won't have heard of that project," Anin said heavily. "His heart's elsewhere."

"He wouldn't have any business getting riled up even if he had," put in Nakona. "I had way more worshipers in Lotus Estuary than he did. If anyone has business throwing a tantrum over that development, it's me, and I—"

"Hold up. Hold up one minute," said Kadiuk, pulling his curved spine surprisingly straight. "Lotus Estuary was my followers' fishing grounds."

"With those little shallow-draft, shore-hugging fishing boats?" Nakona taunted, a wicked smile on her lips.

"Your followers were always so busy chasing the waves in those ridiculous outriggers that they missed the catch close to home," Kadiuk retorted. "My devotees would watch yours and laugh."

"Now, now, now," said Malirin, raising a hand. "There's a way to solve this dispute." And in a graceful gesture, his hand swept down to the tile table.

"Huh. It's practically settled already," Nakona muttered. She turned peremptorily to Mr. Tamlo. "I'm going to need another strawberry juice if I have to indulge this nonsense through another round." Her pleased face belied her grumpy words. Mr. Tamlo handed her a cone-shaped paper cup filled with a thick, red juice. The other retired gods put in their requests, and he filled those too, and soon the four were deep into the next round of tiles. I watched for a while, then excused myself and set off for Sweet Harbor Community Apartments West Branch. The retired Sweet Harbor gods live in Building 2, on the fourth floor, high enough up to catch a glimpse of the sea glinting silver on the horizon, out where the coastline is now.

Ms. Bama, one of Laloran-morna's Compassionate Care attendants, answered the door when I knocked. She dropped her head respectfully, then led me to an inner room where a hospital bed had been raised as high as it would go so that the mattress was level with an open window. A mat woven of rushes—traditional bedding—had been laid on top of the sheets, and Laloran-morna reclined on that, his face toward the window and the sticky breeze that nudged the brass wind chimes hanging there. At my approach he rolled round. A thin, clear tube snaked from an oxygen concentrator beside the bed up over his left shoulder and into his nostrils.

"Ah, Sweeting. Good to see you," he rasped. "You have to talk some sense into the mortals at Compassionate Care. They haven't let me go down to the park for days, and—" He paused, breathless, made the joke he always makes—that somehow when I decommissioned him, he ended up with gills instead of proper lungs—and then continued. "—And besides that, I really need to get to the water's edge."

Ms. Bama clasped her hands. "I've tried to explain about the air quality, and about the difficulty of taking all this downstairs and outside," she said, clearly torn between a desire to accommodate Laloran-morna and her duties as Compassionate Care team member. "There's only ever one—at most two—of us here at a time, and the holy one doesn't have the strength to walk..."

I was touched that she called him "the holy one" — it marked her as from the area: back in the day her family must have been among the faithful.

"I can walk. Just watch," insisted Laloran-morna, struggling to sit up. Ms. Bama hurried to his side, providing an arm for him to grasp as he swung his legs over the side of the bed. He paused again, his shoulders — wide, yet so skinny now — rising and falling with each effortful breath as he recovered from even that exertion.

"Maybe I'm not quite up to it, after all. Not at the moment," he muttered, and seawater bloomed like a sweat stain through the fabric of his pajama shirt, puddling briefly on the rush mat before sinking through the weave and into the mattress below. I took his free hand in mine, squeezed it tight.

"We'll find a way," I assured him, sending what I hoped would be a reassuring look Ms. Bama's way, too. I'd talk to the people at the Ministry, see if there was any discretionary funding that could pay for some extra staffing.

"Could you do me a favor?" Laloran-morna asked abruptly. "In the meantime?"

"Of course."

"The cup you made me." He indicated with his chin where it sat on the window ledge, next to a glass pitcher of water. I felt equal parts embarrassment and pleasure, as you might if a parent or grandparent proudly brings out ancient schoolwork from your childhood. I hadn't made the cup, had merely painted a glaze pattern on an unglazed piece which the shopkeeper then fired, but the pattern was the various knots associated with Laloran-morna—knots that his followers in past eras had woven into their fishing nets to assure a good catch. I had given him the cup on the first anniversary of his decommissioning.

"Can you take it out to the water? And bring palm wine. And say a prayer. Dedicate it to my love. Tell her I'm sorry not to be there. This separation—" He shook his head. "It's a bad thing. I miss her." Then, more forcefully, "Always."

Ms. Bama's eyes widened and met mine. She must have grown up with the same stories of Laloran-morna's stormy love life as I had—mortals, divinities, even the occasional voluptuous cloud or great fish. But that had been in his days as a god. Could he have kindled a romance since retiring? Was this what Anin had been talking about—was it the reason why Laloran-morna always stole away at this time of year?

But then again, don't lovers want to see their beloved more than once a year? Not that I'd know from experience. I've kept pretty fiercely to myself all my life. I prefer the company of divinities—decommissioned or about to be decommissioned—to that of most people.

And Laloran-morna said to say a prayer and to accompany it with wine—that's a ritual for the dead. So was the remembrance for a past lover? If so, which one?

"What name should I speak?" I asked.

"Ehh, we have so many for each other. Sometimes she calls me Lagoonfire because I bring her that soft fire on my warm waves. And I call her Goblet because she receives." His wheezy laugh became a cough.

At the mention of lagoonfire, my fingers and toes tingled. So this dedication was indeed the secret business Anin had mentioned.

"All right," I began, but Laloran-morna wasn't finished.

"Lotus Estuary," he said, handing me the cup with shaking hands. "Do it there."

Now my whole body was tingling.

"Lo-Lotus Estuary is—there isn't an estuary anymore," I stuttered. "It's gone—part of a new development." I held my breath, watching him.

"What? No Lotus Estuary? No. No, no, no." He shook his head, back and forth, back and forth, with each negation. "I knew it was changing. I saw the river move and land appear here and open sea there—places change over time. But it can't be gone entirely..." Another sheen of seawater formed on him, becoming spray in a gust of wind that pushed in through the open window.

So he hadn't known.

"But *she* still is," he said, suddenly still. "She still *is*. So please. Find water someplace near—near to her."

Gripping Ms. Bama's arm more tightly, he lifted his legs onto his rush mat and lay back down.

I kissed him on the forehead.

"I'll do it now," I said. "Rest well, Grandfather." It's presumptuous, but I do call him that. Ms. Bana and I exchanged a wordless goodbye, and I headed out.

As I sat on a midafternoon bus to the Daybreak Ventures construction area, I planned out a message to Five, intending to assure her that Laloran-morna had nothing to do with the flooding at the development site. But I stopped before recording it. True, he'd seemed unaware of how completely Lotus Estuary had vanished and unconcerned about the development—but the fact that he was in the habit of making a secret trip to the area yearly was too much of a coincidence to simply dismiss. I dreaded the thought of the paperwork and explaining I'd have to do if I declared that Laloran-morna was uninvolved only to have later evidence tell a different story. Better to perform Laloran-morna's secret dedication first and see what happened. Maybe after that I'd be able to exonerate Laloran-morna more confidently.

The last three stops on the bus's route were all for the construction project: worker housing, staging area, and sea access. I got off at the terminus, where huge, preformed concrete elements — arches and right-angled pieces, along with what appeared to be segments of pipe — were being unloaded from a barge and into waiting trucks. Further off, another barge was emptying sand along the shoreline.

The bus turned and headed back toward civilization, splashing water out of the ruts it and other vehicles had formed on this last, unpaved stretch of road. The faded schedule posted on the plastiglass wall of the bus shelter promised another would come in half an hour and that service would continue at that frequency until the early evening. Old love songs, their bass notes stripped away by whatever poor-quality device was broadcasting them, were drifting lazily from a kiosk a few steps away from the shelter.

One of the other passengers — some sort of project administrator by the look of her — had lingered at the bus stop. "Are you a reporter?" she asked, squinting at me suspiciously.

"I'm from the Ministry of Divinities," I replied. "I'm here because of the seawater incursion."

Her eyebrows lifted skeptically. "I thought any kind of divine action had already been ruled out. All the rites for all the relevant Abstractions have been observed — Engineering, Marine Ecology, Harmonious Development —" She rattled off a few more of the Abstractions that the Ministry of Divinities favors these days over the old, named deities, and then added, "We even said prayers for the old Sweet Harbor gods. I know they've all been decommissioned, but you know. Just to be safe."

I frowned. The woman probably didn't know she was admitting to breaking the law. Not that I intended to say anything to Five or anyone else at the Ministry, but saying prayers to a decommissioned god is a punishable offense. If too many people do it, the god can end up being redeified. I felt a rush of affection for the Sweet Harbor gods. What if they *could* be redeified?

But no. Sweet Harbor isn't what it once was. There's no harbor anymore, for one thing, so no fishing boats, no small-scale coastal traders. The crowded harborside neighborhoods were all razed and redeveloped three decades and more ago. There's no community left to worship the Sweet Harbor gods, so they won't be coming back — despite Daybreak Ventures' pro forma prayer.

"Anyway," the woman was saying, "that's who I think is behind it. Somehow. Let Civil Order question them — that'll sort things out."

In my reverie, I had missed who exactly it was that this woman thought Civil Order should be questioning, but I had a dedication to perform, so I just nodded, maintaining what I hoped was an expression of thoughtful seriousness. Apparently satisfied with our exchange, the woman took her leave and walked off briskly in the direction of the barge. I lingered at the bus stop; I needed to head for the shoreline too, but I didn't want to follow the woman too closely. I poked my head in at the kiosk—there was the radio I had heard, a tiny plastic thing in the shape of the cartoon mongoose hero of a children's daily animation. But no one was there to sell the brightly packaged snacks and drinks neatly displayed on the back wall and sides of the kiosk. I went around back—still no one in evidence—and from there made my way to the water.

Out along the horizon, bruise-colored cloud towers were drifting across more and more of the sky, and the breeze was picking up. It would be raining soon. I took off my shoes and put them in my bag, then rolled up my trousers and began walking along the water's edge, away from Daybreak Ventures' barges, letting the surf spill over my feet. Very soon the sand ran out, giving way to fine silt that my feet sank into up past my ankles. Disconcerted, I scrambled out of reach of the waves. Here and there mangrove shoots dotted the ground, both above and below the tideline. I had to pick my way among them carefully. Tiny crabs—Kadiuk's children, back when

Kadiuk was a god — sped away from each footstep I took. Looking around, I realized I was on a narrow spit of land, a thin finger extending into the sea. Scattered sparsely along its length were older-sibling trees of the shoots I was trying not to trip over. I could see through their leaves to distant New Harbor, the capital's shipping hub. Even from here, the big cargo ships and the massive cranes that unloaded them were visible.

This narrow stretch of land had neither been smothered in imported sand nor dredged out of existence to accommodate giant ships. Although I couldn't pretend it bore much resemblance to Lotus Estuary back in the day, at least it had a hint of wildness about it. A scattering of mangroves and an abundance of crabs were better than nothing. I wondered briefly about lagoonfire — were there any tiny bioluminescent creatures in the water? During the day it was impossible to tell, but whether there were or not, this would have to be the place for the dedication.

I opened my bag and took out Laloran-morna's cup, along with the palm wine I'd picked up near Laloran-morna's apartment block. It was a tiny, overpriced bottle whose fancy label declared its high-society aspirations. Too bad I couldn't have gotten something distilled in a village somewhere — that's the sort of thing Laloran-morna surely had in mind — but there's no such village within a day's journey of the capital. However pretentious it was, at least the little bottle contained actual palm wine and not one of those fermentations of grain or fruit.

I prepared to pour the wine into the cup, but senses honed by years of experience working with divinities told me there was a presence nearby.

"Hello?" I called out.

Rustling—someone or something moving away, rapidly.

"Hello?" I called again, following the sound with my eyes. The approaching cloudburst had covered the sun; there were no camouflaging dapples to hide in. My eyes met those of a man about my age—an alert, wary gaze in a sweaty face, beneath thick, wild hair. He wore the short-sleeved white shirt of a secondary school teacher or a low-level municipal employee. *Or maybe,* I thought, remembering the woman from the bus, *he's a journalist.*

"Are you from the media?" I asked.

"No," he replied. "Are you from the—" He'd been giving me the same lookover I'd just given him, and now his eyes widened as they took in the cup in my hand.

"That cup! Do you know what that pattern means?" As if my awkward artwork might actually be a secret code.

"Well yes, I do," I said. "I painted it. They're knots for the old Sweet Harbor god Laloran-morna. Unless you know of some other meaning?"

He laughed, all signs of wariness melting away. "No, that's all I meant," he said. "It's just an odd coincidence, because—well, never mind about that. But I'm surprised. Not many people know the old Sweet Harbor gods. Did you grow up in the area? I mean, before all the redevelopment and..." A wave of the hand to refer to the displacement that had accompanied that redevelopment, which had happened when I'd been very young. No one who lived through that likes to talk about it, but for me it's almost a physical inability.

"My grandparents did," I said, deflecting. "They told me all the old stories."

"Mine too." Open, friendly—and we shared the Sweet Harbor gods. Something inside me unlocked, and before I knew it, I was saying, "I'm performing a dedication."

The man's eyebrows shot up. "Here? This land is all under development. Daybreak Ventures doesn't like trespassers."

"Which is why you were hiding in the undergrowth," I said, raising an eyebrow of my own.

He laughed again, but now the wariness was back.

"That's—well, that's complicated. Maybe first we should do introductions. I'm Ninin Ateni—please call me Ateni. I teach ancient history and historical excavations at Bountiful Palms Institute of Lifelong Education. And you?"

Before I could decide how to answer that question, the first few drops of threatened rain speckled the ground, followed by more, and soon it was sheeting down. Ateni and I sought cover where the mangroves grew thickest, but none of the trees were big enough to offer much shelter, and soon we were both soaked.

"It'll pass soon enough," Ateni said with a shrug. It's a standard part of rainy season small talk to complain about being caught in a cloudburst; Ateni's equanimity was refreshing.

And then the sun returned in full force, drawing mist up from the ground all around us and from our sodden clothes. It was clammy and uncomfortable—but also unearthly, beautiful. I turned slowly, letting my arms pass through the glowing streamers. So soon they would fade away, but in that moment, it was like being among celestial beings, clothed in light. I caught sight of Ateni's face, lips parted, eyes shining. Yes, this was better, much better, for a dedication to Laloran-morna's unknown love. I returned to the water's edge and poured the palm wine, Ateni and the ghostly curls of mist my silent witnesses.

"I greet you, Goblet, beloved of Laloran-morna, whom you call Lagoonfire. The god remembers you and salutes you with this cup of wine. His heart is heavy because he cannot stand here himself."

I poured it into the surf, which raced away, then rushed back. The mist was thinning. I looked for a sign, anything I could share with Laloran-morna later about how his dedication was received, but there was nothing.

"That was beautiful," Ateni said presently. "But wasn't Laloran-morna decommissioned years ago? I thought worship of decommissioned gods was a no-no. Not that performing a dedication for a god is the same as worship, I suppose," he added hastily.

"I wasn't doing it for the god. I was doing it for the man." I replied. "He's still alive as a mortal, but he's very ill. Apparently he was in the habit of performing this dedication yearly, but this year he isn't able to, so I offered."

"You? You know him?"

"I decommissioned him. We've been friends ever since."

"You're a decommissioner? You work for the Ministry of Divinities?" The last words came out in a squeak. Ateni's eyes searched out and found the Ministry badge on my shirt, then grew so wide I could see the whites encircling his irises.

"No need to panic," I said, despite a vicarious sense of alarm. "It's not like I'm with Civil Order or anything. The Ministry of Divinities very rarely hassles mortals."

He nodded, head down. He seemed far from reassured.

"I'm a trespasser, remember? You told me so yourself," I said. "So I'm hardly in a position to make any trouble. We're in this together."

He thrust his hands in his pockets. "But you're not banned from the grounds."

"And you are? How did that happen?" I stole a quick look at the sky. Still fresh-scrubbed blue above us, but the next dark clouds were already visible on the horizon. "Tell me on the way back to the bus."

He didn't answer, and when I took a few steps back along the spit, he made no move to follow.

"You're not coming?" I asked.

"I didn't come by bus. I have a moto-canoe over there," he said diffidently, pointing through the trees to the other side of the spit.

A chill moved up my spine. This was a level of covert activity that made his ban from the Daybreak Ventures' property seem more significant and more ominous. My unease must have shown on my face, because he quickly added, "I can explain. I'll walk you back to the bus—so long as you don't mind my ducking out of sight if we see anyone."

I nodded.

"But can you tell me your name? You never introduced yourself."

I had decided on my answer.

"You can call me Sweeting," I said.

Ateni cocked his head quizzically, but I didn't volunteer anything more.

"All right, Sweeting it is."

On our way back, Ateni told me his story.

"My students are all adults with jobs," he began. "They're never going to become professional historical excavators, but they're interested in the past. When major construction is set to happen someplace, I always see if I can get permission to dig there. We usually find something. It might just be old fizz bottles, but even those can be interesting to uncover. But sometimes we find older things, old coins ... sometimes pottery fragments.

"I got permission from Daybreak Ventures to dig on the only remaining bit of estuary before the rains came. I wasn't expecting we'd find much—a historical excavation team from Polity Central University had already been through the area—but our site wasn't near any of theirs, and I thought just maybe we'd get lucky. Maybe turn up pilings from old piers or raised houses, maybe some storage vessels.

"But we found something much bigger. I—maybe I got ahead of myself, but I wanted to make sure the story was heard, so I called a press conference, and—but—" He shook his head and gestured with his hand, as if waving something away.

"But what?" I prompted. "And what was the discovery?"

"Knots, Laloran-morna knots, like the pattern on your cup. Carved into stones."

"Big ones? From a structure? They could have been part of an old shrine."

Ateni was shaking his head. "They weren't for building with— They have, how can I describe it, something like a ring carved into the top of them, and they're rounded. You could thread thick rope through them—they're like giant beads. And they're very, very old. From before the Sea Travelers settled here or the Inland Peoples came coastward. I believe the stones are Mudhugger artifacts."

A laugh bubbled up in me, but at the sight of Ateni's earnest face I swallowed it.

To understand my reaction, you have to understand about the Mudhuggers and the Sea Travelers. The Sea Travelers were the first settlers of the Polity's coastal regions, adventurous seafarers who made their way here from the Coral Archipelagoes some five thousand years ago. Records from their early coastal kingdoms include tales of encounters with magical creatures they called Mudhuggers—child-sized, human-shaped sprites dwelling in the mangrove forests, lagoons, and estuaries. The

Mudhuggers were crafty and potentially dangerous: they could trap a man in the mud, where he would drown as the tide came in. And they were seductive too, despite their small size: Mudhugger women would lure Sea Traveler men into their beds in the tidal flotsam, and Mudhugger men would transform themselves into tiny paddling deer, sneak into Sea Traveler villages when the men were off fishing, and charm the women with their dainty ways. Then they'd turn back into men and complete the seduction.

But the tales also described the Mudhuggers as fearful: afraid of loud clanging noises, afraid of fire, afraid of the open sea. And they were fragile: if you grabbed a Mudhugger with both your hands, so the stories went, you could snap them in half like a stick of kindling.

Creatures of story. That's what the Mudhuggers were.

"I know what you're thinking," Ateni said, speaking quickly. "But do you know about the discovery of the New Harbor bones? It was about fifteen years ago."

Fifteen years ago, I'd been at university. I cast my mind back, remembered the story. The bones had been uncovered during one of the expansions of New Harbor. They were ancient, two thousand years older than the oldest remnants from any Sea Traveler settlement, and small, like the bones of children on the verge of puberty. When they were discovered, somehow the notion arose that they must belong to Mudhuggers, and the idea captured the popular imagination. *Mudhuggers: no longer myth!* and *The reality behind the fairy tale!* proclaimed the entertainment dailies. But if I recalled correctly, respected researchers had concluded otherwise.

"In the end, didn't they decide that the bones belonged to Sea Travelers? That the discovery just proved Sea Travelers arrived here earlier than previously thought?" I asked.

"No material remains of Sea Traveler culture have ever been found dating earlier than five thousand years ago," Ateni said.

"No remains of Sea Traveler culture … So there are remains of some other culture? Mudhugger culture?" It sounded so strange to say those words: Mudhugger culture.

Ateni raked his hand through his hair. "Nothing definitive," he conceded. "Fire pits, some stone blades. The best evidence is giant shell middens."

"Couldn't all those things just as easily be Sea Traveler remains?" I asked.

"Possibly the first two, but probably not the third. How much do you know about the ancient Sea Travelers?" he asked.

"A bit. Not a whole lot."

"Well, they prided themselves on their fishing. Digging in the mud for clams or plucking mussels off rocks was for the weak and unskilled. It's not that they never ate those things, but they didn't subsist on them. So you don't find huge shell middens at Sea Traveler sites."

I pondered this, wondering how the accepted theory accounted for the giant shell middens — if it acknowledged them at all.

"It's very hard to study something that the academy has decided is nonsense," grumbled Ateni. "Everyone makes excuses for evidence that contradicts the established theory and ignores or mocks alternative theories." He sighed. "I should have known the Polity would jump on any mention of Mudhuggers. They shut down our press conference before we even got to make our announcement, and the next day I was sent notification that Daybreak Ventures was suspending access to the site and that I in particular was banned. Within a week, earthmovers had dumped a hundred tons of fill in the area where we'd been digging."

He hunched his shoulders and dropped his head, so all I could see was the glorious tangle of his hair.

"But look," I said, trying for as conciliatory a tone as possible. "Isn't the fact that the stones have Laloran-morna's knots on them evidence that works in favor of the accepted theory and against yours? The knots decorated fishing nets — different knots for different clans. And the Mudhuggers didn't fish, at least according to the stories.

So wouldn't ancient carvings of the knots support the idea that the Sea Travelers arrived here earlier?"

"Let me ask you a question in return," said Ateni, looking up. "Did the Sea Travelers worship Laloran-morna before they arrived here? Was he worshiped back in the Coral Archipelagoes?"

"Yes, he was one of the gods who arrived with the Sea Travelers."

"All right. Next question: is there any evidence of Laloran-morna knots in the Coral Archipelagoes?"

"I don't really know. I only know about him here."

"I don't know either, but it's what I'm going to research next, and I'm betting anything that the answer is no. I bet those knots don't become associated with Laloran-morna until after he comes to our shores."

"So you think Laloran-morna—or his followers—learned of the knots from the Mudhuggers? Even though the Mudhuggers didn't fish?"

"Didn't go out into the sea to fish," Ateni corrected. "They fished by the shores and in the estuaries and lagoons. And nets aren't the only thing the knots could have been used in. Maybe the Mudhuggers used them for something else. And yes, that is what I think." His declaration made me smile. I imagined his students, the cares of their jobs slipping away as they listened to their ardent instructor. He treated me to a bashful grin in return, but then the grin faded. He stopped walking.

"I was wondering," he said, for a moment meeting my eyes, then dropping his gaze.

"Yes?" I said, when he didn't continue. My uneasiness came rushing back. The wind tugged at our sleeves and trousers.

His hand went to his hair again and stayed there, his fingers gripping it.

"It's— Do you suppose you could ask Laloran-morna about the knots? I'll still research, of course. But learning something from him, personally—well, I want to know what he says. What he remembers."

It's not that my uneasiness disappeared, but that when he asked me this—when he invited me to pursue this mystery with him—a warmth expanded through my chest that made the uneasiness seem inconsequential. "Yes, I can do that," I said. "It might tie in to my own assignment. Shall we share contact information?" I raised my wrist so we could exchange particulars unicom to unicom, but Ateni shook his head. "I left mine at home. What with being banned and all, I figured Daybreak Ventures might have asked Civil Order to track me." The bashful grin passed over his face again. "Unicoms aren't great if you want to sneak onto premises you've been banned from." A pause, then he asked, "What's your assignment?"

He'd left his unicom at home? That was a punishable infraction. Compound that with trespassing, and Ateni was potentially making serious trouble for himself. But I pushed those thoughts away and launched into my own story.

"My superiors wanted me to confirm that the inundation at the Daybreak Ventures site wasn't Laloran-morna's fault—and you might think, well why in the world should it be his fault, and that's a complicated story, and I'm ninety-nine percent sure it wasn't, but this love of his, he wanted the dedication performed at Lotus Estuary—basically where the inundation happened—and if she's a ghost, and if she's used to having him come every year, I thought maybe..." I trailed off, aware that I was babbling and that Ateni was looking ill. "Are you all right?" I asked.

"You said inundation. What inundation?" he asked in return.

"Well maybe inundation is overstating it, but seawater found its way into the Daybreak Ventures construction area and caused extensive damage."

"But no one was hurt?" He waited for my answer with his upper lip caught between his teeth.

"Honestly, I don't know, but I assume not, or my superiors would have said." *And probably the job would have gone to someone more senior,* I thought.

"And— And you think the person you performed the dedication for could be responsible?"

"Yes, because ghosts don't like changes. If this Goblet is used to Laloran-morna always coming on a certain date, and suddenly one year he doesn't turn up... I'm not sure a ghost would have the power to cause a seawater incursion—that'll be *my* research task this evening, to find that out—but assuming it's possible, I think maybe she might be responsible. I was hoping I'd get some sign when I made the dedication, but there was nothing." I frowned. "Maybe I should have performed a summoning, but I would have needed divine resin for that."

"Maybe it's my fault," Ateni said, barely audible. "Maybe I'm the one who angered the ghost."

"Why would you think that?"

"After our press conference was shut down, we were escorted off the premises, but I came back. After dark, by moto-canoe. I looped a rope through a knot stone's ring and then dragged it to that spit of land where we met. You've got to understand, I didn't want the stones to be lost forever, and they would have been! Then I went back and did the same thing with another—it was killing the canoe's motor; the stones are like anchors. I managed to drag a third away before the motor died altogether. It's a good thing there was a paddle for backup, or I'd have stranded myself." He paused. "But what I did... If ghosts dislike changes, do you think moving the knot stones could be what upset Goblet?"

"Angry about a few stones — when Daybreak Ventures' dredging and reclamation work is altering the entire coastline? It's got to be their activities that have upset her." But even as I spoke, doubt was creeping into my mind. Ateni, meanwhile, looked unconvinced — and miserable.

"All right," I admitted. "Maybe it's possible, but I don't think it's likely. We need to know more about her, so we can understand her motivation — if she's even the one behind the flooding. Maybe in the end it'll turn out to have been an engineering flaw after all."

One corner of Ateni's mouth lifted in the smallest of half smiles.

"Maybe," he said.

"Don't worry," I said, surprising myself with my own assurance. "Even if for some reason it does turn out to be the stones' removal that caused the flooding, we can fix things."

A muscle twitched along Ateni's jawline, and he closed his eyes. "I'm not returning the stones."

"I was thinking more along the lines of a rite of expiation and exorcism," I said.

His eyes flew open. "There's a protocol like that?"

I nodded, and I could almost see the weight lifting from him.

We resumed walking, but very soon the kiosk by the bus stop came into view, and Ateni's pace slowed once again.

"I'd better leave you here," he said, eyes on the kiosk. A man's voice, singing along with the radio, floated out toward us. "I really shouldn't let anyone see me." He dipped his head farewell, and I returned the gesture. Then he backed away, and with a last glance at the kiosk, turned and loped off in the direction of the mangrove spit.

The wind was rising again, which meant the next downpour was only minutes away. My stomach rumbled. I hadn't stopped to eat after visiting Laloran-morna, and it had been several hours since my mango drink with the other Sweet Harbor gods. I hurried toward the kiosk. The proprietor, a sinewy old man wearing a checked waist wrap and a bright pink T-shirt with a radio station logo on it, was standing in the entrance way. He stopped singing and nodded a welcome.

"What can I get you?" he asked.

I picked out a couple of packets of snacks and a can of chilled tea under his appraising gaze.

"You from Daybreak?" he asked as I paid.

"No, I'm from the Ministry of Divinities," I said, unsettled by the man's scrutiny. "I'm here on official business," I added, and instantly felt frustrated with myself. I didn't need to justify my presence to this man.

"Is that so? The Ministry of Divinities, eh?"

Did he disbelieve me? My badge was right there on my chest.

"There's been troublemakers here," the man said in confidential tones. "The bosses have been in a state, but it'll be sorted soon—they know what's what." He tapped his head knowingly. Then, dreamily, "This place is going to be a big resort one day."

I nodded a stiff farewell and made it to the bus shelter just as the skies opened. Through the plastiglass, I could see the man watching me.

Back at Laloran-morna's apartment, bamboo blinds had been lowered over the windows, and the only light came from the flickering screen on which Ms. Bama was watching a melodrama. She had the sound set to intraocular so as not to disturb the retired god. *Sleeping,* she mouthed to me. She smiled and flicked the melodrama off when I set two insta-meals on the table. We ate together without speaking, the hiss of oxygen and Laloran-morna's labored breathing filling our ears.

"If you'd like to leave early, I'll stay here until Mr. Teka arrives," I said in low tones, after we had finished eating. Ms. Bama's shift had officially ended a quarter of an hour ago, but Mr. Teka was often late.

"Are you sure? But no, I shouldn't. What if there's an emergency?"

"It'll be all right, I promise," I said.

She smiled, nodded once, and took her leave. I exhaled deeply. I felt so at home in Laloran-morna's apartment, much more so than in my own quarters. It reminded me of the apartment I'd lived in with my grandparents after we'd been resettled—safe, quiet, modest. I flicked the screen back on again, but kept the sound off. It was Unity Quarter Hour—primary-school children from all over the Polity singing hymns of national commitment together, a mosaic of different-colored uniforms, mouths forming the same shapes, the words inaudible.

"Did you make the dedication?"

I jumped. It was Laloran-morna's raspy voice, loud and clear from the other room. I hurried to his side. He turned his head toward me and opened his eyes a fraction.

"I did."

He reached out a hand, grasped my wrist. "Did she answer? Did she come?"

"No...there was nothing," I said. A film of seawater formed between his hand and my wrist, salty drops spilling to the floor.

"I should have gone," he said, voice desolate. He released me and turned toward the window. "'Bring your warmth,' she says. 'Bless my garden.' Of course I can't, now. Can't bless anything. And what happens when I die? She won't understand. She'll be, she'll be—" He pulled himself up to sitting, then struggled for breath, a hand on his chest.

"I should have brought divine resin beads," I said, my regret a sharp pang as I watched him struggle. "I could have summoned her. I didn't think to! I'm sorry."

Laloran-morna's head bobbed vigorously on his thin neck.

"Oh yes, that incense. I like that stuff. We all do." He squeezed my wrist again, and more seawater spotted the floor. "Can you try again, with the incense? Summon her? Can you decommission her, like you did me?" His eyebrows formed a mountain peak over imploring eyes.

"Ghosts don't need to be decommissioned, but I can perform a rite of expiation and ...unless Goblet isn't a ghost," I said, the hairs on the back of my neck rising as another possibility occurred to me. "Was—*is*—Goblet a deity?" And then, because all the Sweet Harbor gods and goddess are well known and long since accounted for, and because Ateni had filled my head with his wild theories, I asked, "Is she...a Mudhugger deity?"

Laloran-morna snorted, then coughed. I reached for the pitcher on the windowsill and filled his cup. He took it in trembling hands, drank a few sips, then set it down sharply next to the pitcher.

"'Mudhugger'!" he growled. "What kind of a name is that? 'Mudhugger'—would you call the ones that put out to sea 'Waveclingers'? Or the inlanders—are they Dirtgrubbers?"

"I'm sorry," I said, abashed. "It's just a fairy tale name for fairy tale creatures—but you're right, it's rude. But Goblet..." My tongue had become heavy in my mouth. "Is she a goddess? Of real people?"

For the first time that evening, Laloran-morna's face relaxed into a smile.

"Yes, child, real ones. They made the tidal garden. Her garden. You should have seen it, the jade mussels clinging to the rocks and ropes, ruby slenderweed growing in between. They loved me, you know, because of the fire that rides in on my warm waves—did I mention that before? Lagoonfire. Did I tell you?"

"You mentioned it. You said you called her Goblet because she received."

He chuckled, but then his smile faded. "You'll do it? The decommissioning? I don't want her stranded here, alone, after I go." And now tears filled his eyes. "I did her wrong, but I didn't mean to. I'm sorry. So sorry."

"I'm sure you did no such thing," I protested.

With effort, he lowered himself again.

"Just promise me — the decommissioning."

If she can be decommissioned, I'll decommission her, I wanted to say, but before the failing former god, I couldn't hedge.

"I promise," I said.

"Thank you, Sweeting. You're a good girl. I think I'll sleep again. I'm tired." He blinked, and the tears that had brimmed in his eyes threaded down his cheeks.

From the other room came the sound of a perfunctory knock and the door opening. "Hello? Ms. Bama? I'm sorry I'm late!" Mr. Teka spoke in a hushed voice that wouldn't have woken Laloran-morna, had he been asleep. Before either I or the retired god could give an answer, Mr. Teka was in the archway, peering into the sleeping quarters.

"Oh! Ms. Manu! It's late for a visit, isn't it?"

I managed not to grit my teeth. I'll never like hearing my name spoken aloud, but Mr. Teka's not the sort of person I can ask to call me Sweeting.

"Mr. Laloran needs his rest," he was saying. Mr. Teka's eyes took in the seawater on the floor, and he frowned. "You've upset him!"

"No, no, sonny. It's nothing," Laloran-morna muttered, shifting his position. "If you all would take me to the sea, I wouldn't..." He paused to catch his breath. "Wouldn't have to call it to me."

Mr. Teka forced a laugh. "Of course, of course. Well I'll just clean this up, shall I?" And he bustled into the other room to fetch a towel.

"I should be going," I said. "Good night, Mr. Teka. Good night, Grandfather."

Laloran-morna nodded a farewell, his eyelids drifting closed. I hurried through the front room, but something on the muted screen on the table caught my eye — a breaking news story. But it wasn't the dramatic lettering overlaying the live footage that seized my attention — news broadcasts always use that, even when all they're reporting are improvements to a difficult intersection or new regulations for street vendors. No, it was the figure at the center of the screen, familiar to me from posture, from the disorderly hair.

It was Ateni, handcuffed and flanked by uniformed officers of Civil Order. Now my eyes flew back to the headline — "Lifelong Education Instructor Apprehended in Daybreak Ventures Vandalism Case!" Ateni looked straight into the camera, his panic and confusion transmitting directly to all the viewers. To me. My mouth went dry. I backed away from the table and toward the door, reaching for it blindly as on the screen reporters swarmed the owner of the snack kiosk, who was clearly eager to share his thoughts with the entire viewing Polity. And then my hand found the door, and I was outside, facing the night.

I didn't catch a bus or hail a courtesy vehicle. I hurried up an avenue, turned down a side street, then passed through an alley, then up another side street, another alley, paying no attention to my surroundings, my heart pounding so hard my vision pulsed with each beat.

Eventually I found myself climbing the stairs to my apartment, punching in my lock code, letting myself into the darkened space. I pulled the blinds against the nighttime glitter of the capital, turned on a lamp, and collapsed into the corner of my couch. I wanted to make myself a cup of tea, but I couldn't bring myself to get up. I pulled the two photo frames that sat on the side table into my lap and stared at the images: my grandparents' memorial photos, side by side, in one frame, and a snapshot from my childhood in the other. There I was, a sober-faced orphan, flanked by my equally serious grandparents, their arms like sheltering wings around me.

My mother's parents had done such a good job protecting me, raising me, teaching me how to be a good citizen of the Polity. After they did the paperwork to move me from my father's family registry to theirs, teachers stopped raising their eyebrows in shock when they reached my name in roll call. My grandparents never spoke about my mother and father, never mentioned their crimes, just impressed upon me, over and over, that humility and obedience were virtues that anyone — regardless of parentage — could master. And their efforts had been successful: at all the terrifying junctures when my infamous parents might have been chains around my ankles, I had advanced: to secondary school, to a good university, to, of all things, a government post at the Ministry of Divinities. I had never had any encounters with Civil Order — not one.

And now I was most likely the last person to interact with a man accused of a serious crime. *And it's not even his fault — he was just trying to protect some artifacts — and the goddess might have flooded the area even if he hadn't removed them.* If that was even what has happened.

For that matter, why, exactly, did Civil Order think Ateni was to blame in the first place? Even if they knew he removed the knot stones — a crime, to be sure, but not the crime they were accusing him of — they couldn't possibly know about Goblet. As far as I could tell, only I, Ateni, and Laloran-morna knew about her. Without her in the picture, how could Civil Order think Ateni was responsible for the flooding?

I put the photos back on the table, forced myself to my feet, and made that cup of tea. With each sip the tension in my neck and shoulders eased, and soon it was possible to contemplate next steps. I was going to have to go to Civil

Order. I was going to have to explain their mistake and offer the proper solution: a decommissioning. But this thought brought with it a clammy, suffocating sense of terror so overwhelming I nearly dropped the teacup. Flashes of memory—a pat on the cheek, a question overheard: "Are you ready?" And five-year-old me, piping up. *I'm ready, I'm ready too* — unheard, ignored. And then on the airwaves, *Jowa Fen, Jowa Fen, Jowa Fen, murder, mass murder, state menace,* followed by the snap, click, or chime of the broadcast being silenced by my grandmother or grandfather.

And then silence and more silence.

I didn't want to go to Civil Order — but I had to.

But maybe, I thought, stalling, *I should talk to the Ministry first, share what I've learned, explain about needing to perform a decommissioning. For safety — and because I've promised Laloran-morna.*

Checking my unicom, I found a flurry of messages from Five. The first couple questioned why I hadn't yet filed a report. Then there was the third:

Forgo further interrogation of Laloran-morna, it directed. *The culprit in the Daybreak Ventures incident has been apprehended.*

My stomach flip-flopped.

There was also a message from Kele Tailin — Decommissioner Thirty-Three, my colleague:

Still at work, Thirty-Seven? Any time to take in the Art for the Abstractions exhibition tonight? Let me know.

It was a momentary comfort. Tailin was indefatigably friendly in the face of my introversion and willing to accommodate my preference to go by my decommissioner number even in personal interactions — part of my perpetual effort to distance myself from my name.

"Apologies for the late response — problems with my current assignment," I recorded. "Maybe another time, or another exhibition."

To my surprise, an answer came back instantly. *You're working too hard, as always. If the problems are anything I can help with, I'm here. Oh, and the exhibition will be up for a month, so maybe we can go another time.*

It was probably exhaustion and anxiety that caused a lump to form in my throat, listening to that. It was so like Tailin — always kind.

I really had to send a response to Five. Instead, I made another cup of tea, drank it. Bit a thumbnail. Paced the room. Closed my eyes, took a few deep breaths. Then I started recording.

"I suspect Civil Order made the arrest in error. From Laloran-morna's account, I believe a hitherto undocumented divinity may be responsible for Daybreak Ventures' problems."

I waited for several tense moments, but no reply was forthcoming. Of course not: it was late. There'd be no answer until morning. I started getting ready for bed, but the image of Ateni from the news, lost-looking and small between the Civil Order officers, flashed in my mind, and I froze.

"I won't abandon you," I said. Then I started mentally reciting the names of all the deities in the Polity, present and decommissioned, associated with the Abstractions of Courage and Serenity. In that manner I was able to finish preparing for bed, and at some point I drifted to sleep.

Decommissioner Five video-contacted me at daybreak the following morning, before I even have a chance to comb my hair or wash my face.

"I've just been talking with a captain from Civil Order," she said, no preamble, no pleasantries. "It seems someone wearing a Ministry of Divinities badge and matching your description was seen at the Daybreak Ventures site yesterday, talking with the man they took into custody. Was it you?"

Civil Order. Ateni in handcuffs. That touch on my cheek, long ago. There was a roaring in my ears, but I made myself answer.

"Yes, ma'am, but—"

Decommissioner Five leaned forward, her face filling my wall screen.

"Have you had contact with him in the past? Is he an associate of yours?"

"No! Absolutely not. I met him for the first time yesterday."

"Did you know his family was displaced by the Sweet Harbor land redevelopment initiative thirty years ago? Just like yours. Well. Not *just* like, but."

I always wondered how much Decommissioner Five knew about my past, my notorious roots. I had a feeling that Civil Order had filled her in on anything she hadn't known before.

"He mentioned it," I said. "But only in passing—we didn't talk about it."

She pursed her lips, regarding me silently.

"You just happened to run into him," she said at last.

"Yes."

"And why exactly were you on Daybreak Ventures' property in the first place?"

"For the assignment you gave me! To find out if Laloran-morna had anything to do with the flooding!" I explained about his yearly dedication to a secret love and my suspicion that this lover was a lingering deity who had caused the flooding in her disappointment over his absence.

"And so Ateni can't be responsible," I concluded.

Five's eyes closed at the mention of Ateni's name, and when they opened, her expression was grim.

"Mr. Ninin" — she emphasized Ateni's family name — " is responsible." Each syllable as hard edged as if carved in slate. "Civil Order found explosives in his apartment — the same explosives that were used in the Daybreak Ventures incident."

"Explosives? What explosives? You didn't mention anything about explosives when you gave me the assignment —"

"Thirty-Seven."

"And Ateni — Mr. Ninin — I'd swear on the Abstractions of Truth and Justice that he didn't know anything about the flooding. If you could have seen his face when I mentioned it —"

"Thirty-Seven!"

There was much more I wanted to say, but I clamped my mouth shut.

"I didn't know about the explosives, myself, when the request came to look into the incident," Five said. "But that's what the news says now, and that's what the captain

I spoke with said. Civil Order is absolutely sure they have the right man. Do you understand?" She held my gaze.

The roaring was in my ears again.

"Decommissioner Thirty-Seven, I asked you a question."

"I understand," I muttered, and then, because she was still glaring at me, a little louder: "I understand, ma'am."

Her face relaxed. "Good. Now then, while I have you here, why don't you tell me why you think this lover of Laloran-morna's is a deity." Her tone had shifted to one of professional interest, as if the previous grilling hadn't happened, but my thoughts were a shattered mess. I struggled to sort through them and produce a coherent reply.

"Well," I said, "Laloran-morna said she was one. With a garden in Lotus Estuary, and worshipers there."

Decommissioner Five's silence invited me to continue. I sighed.

"That's it," I said. "That's why I think so."

"Don't you think it's more likely that he was simply exaggerating? Remember the story of his lover Ailia? In the *Black Pearl Rhapsodies* Laloran-morna calls her 'my lightning, my comet, my goddess,' but Ailia was as mortal as any of us," Five observed.

I broke eye contact. I couldn't dredge up countering sources and precedents, not after everything that had happened yesterday, not after what Five had just told me. Why was Civil Order insisting that Ateni was the culprit? Didn't they want to find the real reason for the flooding? And why was Five dismissing the possibility of a hitherto unknown goddess?

"It's very unlikely the Ministry has overlooked a Sweet Harbor deity," Five said, as if in answer to my unspoken question, "and even more unlikely that one could survive into the present day solely on the regard of a retired god."

"I know," I said. It occurred to me that Five's past twenty-four hours must have been rivaled my own for stress. She hadn't had complete facts; she'd learned unsettling details about one of her subordinates. And now that subordinate was making melodramatic, unsubstantiated claims. I felt defeated.

Except I had promised Laloran-morna that I would decommission Goblet. I couldn't fail him. And Ateni... With what Laloran-morna had told me, there had to be some way I could clear Ateni's name. I lifted my head. Decommissioner Five was watching me with some concern.

"If there's even a shadow of a chance that there is an overlooked deity, isn't it the job of the Ministry to investigate?" I asked. "Isn't part of the Department of Decommissioning's mission to prevent overlooked deities from making trouble? Not to discount Civil Order's findings in the Daybreak Ventures case, but if there's some lingering, undecommissioned deity around, or even just a resentful ghost, there's a risk of further trouble at the site. Someone could be hurt."

Five was statue-still. I couldn't read her expression.

"There's another thing," I said, ignoring my internal censor's desperate attempts to keep me silent. "Laloran-morna asked me to decommission this former lover."

That broke whatever spell had held Five frozen.

"You will do nothing like that," she snapped. "You're not to go anywhere near the Daybreak Ventures site. Civil Order has already insinuated that you're somehow involved in" — she waved her hand as if batting away flies — "whatever this is. You are not to do anything that would support those insinuations. I have a responsibility to look after your best interests — and the Ministry's standing."

Then came a concession: "Just to be absolutely certain none of Laloran-morna's lovers are deities who have fallen through the cracks, I'll have you, Thirty-Three, and Thirty-Six log all of them and check their attributes. Thirty-Three will have to be in charge for seniority reasons, but determining what attributes to check will be your decision, and you can do a final check on the status judgments. All right?"

"Yes ma'am."

She nodded. "Good. See you in the office shortly." The wall screen reverted to a default image of birds in flight that I had never bothered to personalize. I continued to stare at it, wishing vaguely for wings. Eventually I roused myself, washed my face, and ten minutes later I was on my way out the door. On the threshold I paused for a moment, surveying my austere quarters. Nothing to see: everything precious to me I kept locked in my head—with the exception of the photos of my grandparents. *Make us proud,* they admonished. My throat constricted. I pulled the door closed and headed to the Ministry.

Tailin and Hena Feshi—Decommissioner Thirty-Six— were already waiting in the conference room Tailin had reserved for us to use when I arrived. They made a startling visual contrast: Tailin tall and bony, with a long face and paler skin than you usually see in the capital region, and Feshi short and rounded, her skin dark and healthy.

"Hello Sae, it's a pleasure to be working with you," Feshi began, her voice warm. "I mean Thirty-Seven," she amended, catching Tailin's frown. One hand flew to the hairband that was holding back her curls, as if to tuck in escapees, though her hair was perfect as it was. "It's a pleasure to be working with you...Thirty-Seven."

Of course Feshi would default to personal names. The three of us were all grade-three decommissioners—no reason for formalities. And of course she'd know my name—it's on the roster right after hers. My grandparents could change me from Jowa Sae to Manu Sae, and I could obscure my identity by using my childhood nickname or my decommissioner number, but in the end, I couldn't hide who I was.

"It's all right; you can call me Sae," I said.

Tailin, who was handing us notepads and styluses, gave me a questioning look. I tipped my head in a minute nod to reassure him.

Feshi laughed awkwardly. "Sae, then. Tailin says we're looking for former lovers of the god Laloran-morna, that there may be one who's an overlooked deity? He said you'll tell us what traits of Laloran-morna's lovers we should search on." I was grateful, now, that Five had picked her for this assignment. I sensed none of the scorn or pity from her that I sometimes felt from the other young grade threes, who saw in me a woman almost a decade older than they were whose career had stalled. No one treated Tailin that way; everyone knew he turned down promotions because he liked archival work. I, on the other hand, just looked stuck, although the truth was that I too was happy where I was, overlooked and unremarked upon.

But what search terms to give to Feshi and Tailin? "We should limit the search to any lovers connected with Lotus Estuary," I said. "Other than that...lagoonfire, and gardens, tidal gardens. And jade mussels, and..." I struggled to remember the particulars that Laloran-morna had mentioned. "And ruby slenderweed, and the name 'Goblet.' Laloran-morna called her Goblet." *And Laloran-morna knots*, I thought of adding, but then thought better of it. I could search on that myself.

"Tidal gardens? Like fish husbandry? Did they have fish husbandry back when the Sweet Harbor gods were active?" Feshi asked.

"I don't think tidal gardens mean fish husbandry," I said, "but I'm not sure what they do mean. Maybe check mention of any gardens in, by, or near Lotus Estuary."

I was not at all surprised when, by the noon hour, we hadn't turned up anything I considered useful. There was the famous *Tale of the Stolen Goblet*, in which a thief charmed Laloran-morna into sending his waves into the treasure house of one of the many Sea Traveler kings and then swam in and stole a precious cup for a rival king to whom the thief owed a debt of gratitude for saving her life. There was a record of a rivalry between Kadiuk and Laloran-morna for the affections of a girl from a village by Lotus Estuary: Laloran-morna brought her a stack of jade mussels from the estuary, but in each one the girl opened she found a little pea crab, child of Kadiuk. This clever girl thanked both the gods for their bounty — to be enjoyed by all the guests at her wedding to her sweetheart, a boy from the same village.

Then there was something Feshi had found, mention of a brief romance between Laloran-morna and a goddess of the northern current, but the source of the story was a record from Misty Isthmus, which was nowhere near Lotus Estuary, and the romance itself occurred out on the wild ocean waters. But Feshi was excited by the finding. "The goddess was really short-lived," she said. "Her worship only appears in the record 700 years ago, and it fades away about 150 years later. But she's not on the roster of decommissioned deities — she was never officially retired!"

I was only half paying attention. My thoughts were on what I had discovered about worship of Laloran-morna in the Coral Archipelagos, back in ancient days, before the archipelagos were colonized by the fiercely monotheistic Tessani Union. Those low-lying islands rose barely a man's height above the water, so for the islanders of long ago, the storms that rode in on Laloran-morna's warm waves had been a source of terror, and the god himself had, like the god of storms, been a figure of menace to be propitiated. They had no affectionate tales about him — and there were no mentions of Laloran-morna knots.

"Sae?" Feshi was waiting for my response, and behind her, so was Tailin. I was at a loss — Feshi's goddess was clearly not Laloran-morna's Goblet, so what was there to say?

"She does sound like an interesting case," I began — that much was true, and in other circumstances I'd be intrigued — "but I don't think she's relevant for the current investigation."

Feshi's face fell.

"Regardless of its relevance for Sae's search, it's an excellent find," Tailin said quickly. "If this goddess was never officially decommissioned, she'll need to be. These are just the sorts of loose ends that Five is eager to tidy up."

Feshi shot him a grateful look.

"Why don't you get yourself something to eat," he suggested to her. "We can continue the search and discuss next steps after the noon meal."

Feshi nodded. "Can I bring you back anything? And you too, Sae — would you like anything?"

"You can bring us both tea," Tailin said, before I could decline the offer. Feshi nodded once, managed a smile, and left the room.

"You need to be more diplomatic," Tailin said, once we were alone. "Feshi likes you." He didn't need to add that this wasn't true of many of our colleagues. I felt a prick of shame, but it was nothing to the impatience that had me nearly jumping out of my skin.

"It's just that I'm looking for a particular goddess whom Laloran-morna mentioned to me — it's not the sort of thing where a substitute's going to be just as good," I said. "And Feshi's goddess isn't the one I'm looking for — I'm sure of it."

"All right. The discovery isn't good for you, personally, but at least it's a return on the investment of time and labor that Five authorized — that she authorized on your behalf, right? Maybe this will change in the afternoon, but as it stands now, if it weren't for Feshi's discovery, we'd have nothing at all to show for our efforts, and Five would have a hard time defending the allocation of research hours. Feshi's goddess pays for your search time. And anyway, it's not like the goddess you're looking for is the only potential troublemaker out there — you know any undecommissioned deity is a potential headache. Worse than neglected ancestors or ghosts with grievances... What's this?"

He'd noticed the article displayed on my work console. "The Coral Archipelagos? You didn't mention them as a relevant factor." He glanced at the search field, where "Laloran-morna knots" was displaying zero returns. "Why Laloran-morna knots?"

Tailin was the only person in the world I counted as a friend — not including former divinities — and yet when I tried to find the words and courage to explain, I couldn't.

"The man they detained in the Daybreak Ventures case," Tailin said presently. "He had an instructor's license, but it turns out he's one of those off-center types who believe Mudhuggers were a historical people. He took his unsuspecting students on a dig at the Daybreak Ventures site and tried to get airtime to claim some artifacts that turned up were made by Mudhuggers. The artifacts were stones, stones with Laloran-morna knots inscribed on them."

He hesitated, but when I didn't speak, he continued.

"And you met him, didn't you. Yesterday. When you were on assignment."

So he'd heard about that. What else had Five told him?

"Yes," I said.

"And now, suddenly, while we're trying to find this goddess you're very particular about, you're spending time researching Laloran-morna knots? Is it because of that man?"

I dismissed the article and returned to the query portal while I tried to think of a reply that would be both safe and truthful.

"Thirty-Seven?" Tailin's voice was pleading.

"Aten... Mr. Ninin makes the Mudhugger theory sound not quite so outlandish. And the stones he found, with the Laloran-morna knots on them—I think they may have a connection to the goddess I'm looking for—and to the flooding at Daybreak Ventures."

An incredulous laugh burst from Tailin.

"Well yes, there's a connection to the flooding. *He's* the connection. He planted the bomb that caused it!"

"Does that seem plausible to you?" I challenged. "That a historical excavator would do something that could damage the site he's been excavating?"

"Maybe? If he were prone to crackpot theories and was angry enough when they were ignored? Or if he's a retrogressivist, which is what the news is saying—that he's against development initiatives and social improvements. Why would you defend someone like that?"

"I think the goddess I'm searching for may have been a Mudhugger goddess," I blurted out.

Tailin pressed the heels of his hands against his eyes. "I can't believe this," he said in strangled tones.

I plunged ahead. "Did you know they didn't have the tradition of special clan knots in nets in the Coral Archipelagos? That tradition only grew up around Laloran-morna after the Sea Travelers arrived here."

"So it grew up here—so what? Cultures change."

"But what if it changed because of contact with a people here who were already using the knots—somehow? People who didn't fish but tended gardens of jade mussels and—"

"Ruby slenderweed," he finished, with a resigned sigh.

"Yes. I think Goblet might have been worshiped by those people. Laloran-morna said the garden was hers."

"But there's no evidence of any coastal people in these areas prior to the Sea Travelers' arrival."

I decided not to bring up the shell middens. Instead I asked, "What about the stories of the Mudhuggers? Aren't they a kind of evidence?"

"Not in the absence of something to confirm them—unless you want us to believe all fairy tales are actually histories."

"Well no, but—"

"And think about how the Mudhuggers get described in those tales. They're promiscuous, sly, cowardly. Fragile. It's not how anyone would describe themselves—or someone they respected. Would you want to be described that way?"

"How is that relevant?" I asked.

"Isn't it relevant? For the Polity's foundational story? There are the Inland Peoples and the Sea Travelers, yes? They may have fought like tigers when they first came in contact, but the tales on both sides of the ancient record emphasize bravery, loyalty, devotion, honor. And now you're suggesting we wedge a third people into the record? Oversexed, cowardly sneaks?"

"Well, that's probably not how the Mudhuggers would have described themselves—those are the Sea Travelers' descriptions of them."

"Which shows the Sea Travelers didn't think much of them. Think about the Sea Travelers' stories about the Inland Peoples — or the reverse. Whatever battle narratives you look at, the accounts always acknowledge the fearsomeness — which is to say, the worthiness — of the enemy, right? And sometimes even their nobility — think of the *Lament of the Ebony Spear*, King Ketak mourning over the body of his enemy's son."

"I don't know... I think sometimes if you fear something, you belittle it." I was recalling the history behind a decommissioning case I'd had recently, in which a potentially threatening deity had been emasculated by the disparaging framing of his godhead.

"The stories say you could break the Mudhuggers with your bare hands!" Tailin exclaimed. "How does that indicate fear? And here's another thing: if they were that easily dispatched — even if it's a metaphor, or an exaggeration, that's what that indicates, right? If they were that easily dispatched, what do you suppose became of them?"

It wasn't really a question. The Sea Travelers and the Inland Peoples had been well matched, but we both knew about first contacts where that hadn't been the case. The Tessani Union's takeover of the Coral Archipelagos, the Transoceanic Trading Fellowship's first arrival on the Great Western Continent. Colonization, obliteration from violence or disease, enslavement. Those were all part of the historical record — elsewhere.

We sat in silence a moment, and then Tailin said, "Whatever the answer is, I don't think it's something that the Committee on Thought Orthodoxy would be eager to incorporate into the Polity's history, any more than the Department of Ancestors is going to want to tell people their Firsts may have been promiscuous scaredy-cats. Too demoralizing."

"If something is true, though," I said slowly. "Then the Polity should face it — shouldn't it? 'Helpful critique weeds out bad practice so the Polity flourishes,'" I quoted. It's a favorite Thought Orthodoxy maxim.

Tailin shook his head. "'Beware the fools who cut fruiting branches when pruning; they will destroy the orchard,'" he quoted back. "We're talking about something that happened thousands of years ago — if it even happened at all, if such a people ever really existed. What's the point of resurrecting a people whom no one has missed, when their resurrection can only cause harm?"

"To prevent their goddess from destroying a development site?"

Tailin grinned in spite of himself. "You win points for persistence, Thirty-Seven."

I pressed my advantage. "Will you give me leave to go ask Laloran-morna some more questions? I think I need — we need — more details, things only he can tell us."

Tailin regarded me in silence for a long moment. "All right. On one condition," he said.

"What?"

"I want you to think of this goddess as a Sea Traveler deity. When you're writing up notes of your conversation with Laloran-morna, that's what you'll do. All right? No mention of Mudhuggers. Do you promise?"

"But if — "

"No buts — that's the deal."

Tailin's firmness is famous in the Ministry. I wasn't going to beg or bargain a better arrangement out of him, and I needed to see Laloran-morna. I bowed my head in acknowledgement.

The door to Laloran-morna's apartment was shut and locked, and a query to Ms. Bama returned this message:

The holy one had a crisis this morning; we are at hospital. Should be back at home by evening. He wants to see you, and he keeps talking about getting to the sea.

I had to get him to the sea. It was terribly wrong for him to have been kept from it during this final illness. Warm waves belong to the sea. And if he had been able to get to the sea earlier... My thoughts flew to Goblet. If only he had been able to make the dedication himself—maybe nothing that was happening now would have come to pass.

But what you promised him was the decommissioning, I reminded myself. And for that to happen, I still needed more information about Goblet—which Laloran-morna was in no condition to provide right now. And might never be. I thought over the stories Tailin, Feshi, and I had uncovered so far that had mentioned Lotus Estuary. There was the one where Kadiuk and Laloran-morna had both been tricked by the village girl—and hadn't Kadiuk said something about Lotus Estuary being his followers' fishing grounds? Clinging to the slim hope that Kadiuk might know something about Laloran-morna's secret love, I made my way to the Promise of Unity Primary School Park.

The retired Sweet Harbor gods had been lured away from the tile tables by a swarm of children from the primary school who had been brought to the park with boxes of winged seeds from the lobe-leafed gourd vine. Their teacher was directing them to throw the seeds into the air, but the children needed no prompting—they were flinging the seeds skyward with great shouts and then cooing and cheering as the seeds drifted like birds on the faintest currents. They had painted designs on the papery wings: splashes of bright blue, orange, vivid green, scarlet.

"Mine's winning! Mine's winning!" one boy was exclaiming in a high, thin voice.

Kadiuk chuckled. "The boy's right. Look—his bird's still flying." And he pointed a gnarled finger at one seed whose wings sported purple stripes. As I watched, the winged seed floated gracefully to the ground.

"But that one flew further, even if it didn't fly as long," Nakona observed, nodding toward one with yellow starbursts on each wing that had landed at the far end of the park. "I think that one should be the winner." She shot Kadiuk a sidelong glance, but he didn't take the bait. Instead he turned to me.

"Sweeting!" That warm, gravelly voice—gnarled like his fingers. The others' attention all turned my way and they clustered round, the children and their seed-birds forgotten.

"Do you have word about Lolo?" Anin asked.

"Look at her face," Malirin said. "You can see it's nothing good."

"You can't let Lolo's mortal life end four floors up in a steel-and-concrete box," Anin pleaded.

Nakona heaved a sigh. "This dying business. It makes me wish we all could've just faded away—like we would have, if left in peace, I might add!—instead of being decommissioned."

It was anticipation of grief, I told myself, that was making Nakona question decommissioning. She more than any of the others always seemed to be wholeheartedly enjoying her retirement as a mortal. But death is hard.

"I-I do have an idea about getting Lolo to the sea," I said, a plan forming in my head even as I spoke. "But there's something else I need to do for Lolo first, and I need your help. Especially yours, I think, Kadiuk."

"This old crustacean?" Nakona cast a dubious glance in Kadiuk's direction. "Well the old crab can help you back by the tile tables. It's hot, and I want a strawberry juice. I'm getting sweaty. Oi, Mr. Tamlo! Don't go! We're coming!" she hollered, though the juice vendor was showing no signs of leaving.

Back at the tile tables everyone ordered a juice and settled onto the tables' concrete seats.

"So what is it I can do for the god of the warm waves?" Kadiuk asked, taking a sip from his paper cone of guava juice.

"You said Lotus Estuary was your followers' fishing grounds," I began.

Kadiuk nodded. "From the very beginning. The people knew where to find me—me and my children—in the sand and mud, playing with the waves. That's how mortals used to do it around here, you know," he said, turning to the others and adopting a teacherly tone. "Worship the creature and the place. None of this tides-and-waves business."

Nakona snorted.

"Now, now, no need to take offense," Kadiuk said, patting her hand. Nakona whipped it away in a show of mock pique.

"Truly! I'm glad the rest of you showed up," Kadiuk continued, placating. Without deigning to look Kadiuk's way, Nakona slid her hand back across the table and let Kadiuk give it a squeeze.

"Wait. What do you mean, you're glad the rest of them showed up?" I asked. "You all arrived together...didn't you? No? You were always...here?"

Kadiuk took another sip of his juice and nodded.

"If they hadn't come, I might never have discovered another part of myself," Kadiuk said. "The deep-sea crab. What a magnificent child, magnificent sibling." Kadiuk's face was rapt. Then, as if telling me a secret, "Did you know this lot brought their own followers with them? Their followers fished for the deep-sea crab, out in the wide deep sea. When they learned about me, well!" He leaned back on his seat, bracing himself with his arms and pushing out his chest. "They worshiped me, of course—to win favor with the deep-sea crab."

But I barely registered this part of his story. "You were always here," I repeated. "You were here before the rest of the Sweet Harbor gods came. Which means there were people here before they came."

Kadiuk continued as if I hadn't spoken. "Of course it worked the other way too. My followers took to worshiping these upstarts, especially busy Nakona here, always coming and going, and Lolo, since his warm waves—"

"Brought the lagoonfire," I breathed.

"Yes, yes exactly," exclaimed Kadiuk, beaming.

"Well you know how you were telling me about Lolo always going off by himself for a day or two during lagoonfire season? It turns out he was going to Lotus Estuary!" I said.

This news didn't provoke the reaction I had imagined it would.

"Well, he did have followers there," Kadiuk said with a shrug.

"Not as many as I did," Nakona muttered.

"I had propitiators," Anin chimed in. "It comes to the same thing."

"He was meeting someone," I said.

"Of course he was," said Nakona, rolling her eyes.

"That does sound like Lolo," said Malirin with an air of tolerant serenity.

"A deity," I said. I turned to Kadiuk. "Someone like you, someone who was here before these others came."

Kadiuk's brow knit. "Another like me? I don't really remember ..." His age, which he always wore so cavalierly, seemed to fall on him suddenly, curving his spine more, deeply hollowing out his cheeks, dimming his eyes. "But I know there were others... There must have been others..."

"He said he called her Goblet," I said.

"Goblet!" Kadiuk snapped back to himself. "Of course—there was always Goblet! You mean that little upstart god was using his words and touches on *her*?"

"So you remember her? Did she have another name, a truer name—something her followers called her?"

"She was the Goblet!" Kadiuk spread his hands wide. "The Goblet of Life, the Cup of the Sea—it's what we called that place before we called it 'Lotus Estuary.' What kind of name is 'Lotus Estuary,' anyway? Lotuses don't grow in that brine, but we do! Mud crabs, pea crabs, red-clawed crabs...and the others: jade mussels, slenderweed, milkfish, spotted catfish—"

I interrupted the litany. "So Goblet—she's a tutelary goddess? Of Lotus Estuary — of Cup of the Sea?"

"She is the estuary. Was the estuary. She faded away long ago. It became just a place. Just geography." His brows pulled together again. "So how could Lolo have kept on visiting her?"

"I think she didn't fade, not totally. Lolo's regard for her kept her there," I said slowly. "Or sort of there."

"Ughhh, what a nightmare. The positive worst move of a demanding lover," said Nakona, shaking her head.

"I think it's romantic," said Anin, and Malirin nodded agreement.

"Still here," murmured Kadiuk. "But I never felt her. Never knew. She was a mother to us—the crabs, the mussels, the slenderweed… I wish I had known."

"Maybe you can see her tonight. All of you, if you want," I said, meeting eyes with each of the retired deities. "We can make things right for her, and for Lolo." *I hope*, I added silently.

"Really? You'll find a way to bring Lolo to the sea?" Anin asked. A whoop went up from the schoolchildren at the other end of the park, and they surged out the front gate, following their teacher. I quelled my fears and doubts.

"Yes, I really will," I promised.

"Then we'll join you," Kadiuk said, with such finality in his voice that I felt it was time for me to take my leave.

"I have just one more thing I wanted to ask you," I ventured.

Kadiuk raised his eyebrows.

"Cup of the Sea... Did Goblet have a garden there?"

He smiled. "The whole thing is a garden. Was a garden," he said.

"Do you recall rocks in it, rocks with knot patterns on them?"

"Yes, yes of course. Clan markers, for the parts of the garden cultivated by different mortal families. They'd fasten ropes to them, knotted with their family pattern. They'd seed some ropes with slenderweed and others with jade mussels."

A rush of vicarious vindication passed over me, so sharp I nearly gasped.

"Thank you," I said.

I took my leave but didn't head back to the Ministry. Instead I let my feet carry me to Civil Order's West Ward offices, where Ateni was being held. Whatever else happened—and I had plans for quite a few things to happen—I had to let him know he had been right about the knot stones. On the way I sent a message to Ms. Bama, asking her to let me know when she and Laloran-morna were back at his apartment, and a message to Tailin: *Things on this end are taking longer than expected, but I'll be back before closing. And I want to ask you about that exhibition you mentioned yesterday. If you're free tonight, I think I'd like to see it.*

Civil Order's West Ward offices were in a nondescript building just a little past the bustling West Ward train station, in the shadow of Pinnacle Tech's new high-rise and within sight of Polity Central University's West Ward campus. The plaque above the door, bronze, with the Polity's national seal above it, provided the sole accent of grandeur. The very notion of Civil Order was all that was needed to create an accompanying atmosphere of intimidation. The streets in this area were always full, but I had the impression that vehicles became more subdued in their honking and that pedestrians sped up as they passed in front of the offices.

From the other side of the street, I found myself hesitating. Maybe I should just go back to the Ministry. There would surely be some way to get a message to Ateni by official channels and— No. I gritted my teeth and stepped off the curb, joining other pedestrians dodging buses, courtesy vehicles, and delivery trucks.

The door wasn't at street level: there were stairs leading up to it and ramps flanking them. A frontal assault was altogether too daunting. I took the ramp to the right. The doors had long, thin, handles made of amber-colored wood. I pulled one, and heavy as the door was, it swung open smoothly and silently.

The interior reminded me of a train station—one big, high-ceilinged room, with rows of benches on either side of a central aisle. An imposing desk, so high that it required stairs to reach the seat, was over to the right at the other end of the room. Various inspirational or chastising Thought Orthodoxy maxims were impressed into the back wall in gold leaf below an incongruously modern-looking time piece that showed hours, minutes, and seconds in digital form. On the left side of the far wall was an unassuming little door that managed nevertheless to be menacing: behind it lay Civil Order's offices—and its detention cells.

An assortment of people, from adolescents to a grandmotherly-aged woman wearing a crossing-guard's sash, were sitting on the benches. A few looked angry, but most seemed anxious or frightened. At the high desk sat a low-ranking Civil Order officer, a man with hair so short it seemed painted on his head—and also a beard, similarly severely short. Having a thick, full head of hair is a point of vanity for men and women alike in most of the Polity— but not among the ranks of Civil Order. They emulate the austerity of the military.

This man now addressed me. "Do you have a summons? Let me scan your unicom."

"No, I—" My mouth was dry. "I just came... I'm here to—"

"Come here," he ordered.

I came.

"Now show me your unicom."

The desk was so tall that I had to hold my wrist up over my head.

"There's no summons here," he said. "Why are you here?"

"I want to see someone." I swallowed. "Someone in custody."

The officer handed me down a stylus and a small screen. "You'll need to fill out the application on the screen," he said. "It will take about ten days to process, and then we'll give you a date and time."

My heart sank, but I rallied. What I couldn't share with Ateni today, I could share with him before the month was out. Maybe by then the charges against him would even be dropped. I started filling out the form and immediately hit a roadblock.

"It says prisoner number," I said. "But I don't know his prisoner number."

"Name?" the officer queried.

"M-mine, or his?"

"His, of course."

"Ateni, Ninin Ateni." Had the room's cooling system quit? My skin prickled with heat. I had the sense that everyone else in the room was staring at me, but I refused to glance back and see.

"Ohhhhh." The officer drew out the syllable, a long exhale. Now he was standing, gazing down at me avidly. "You're that Ministry of Divinities functionary." Without taking his eyes off me, he spoke into his unicom. "Captain Lotuk, you won't believe who walked in here. Ninin's confederate, the one that woman at Divinities swore up and down had nothing to do with him. She wants to see him!" He couldn't stop staring at my Ministry badge. "How'd you pull it off, Ms. *Jowa*?" he asked, emphasizing the family name, eyes narrowed. Sweat ran down my back beneath the twisted cable of my hair.

"It's Manu," I croaked. "Manu Sae."

He barked a laugh. "Sure. I'd change my name, too."

By then the narrow door at the far side of the wall had opened, and a woman, whom I realized must be Captain Lotuk, had joined us.

"Hello, Ms. Manu," she said. "It's good of you to come in."

"I'm not 'coming in,'" I said, taking a step backward, "I just wanted to see Mr. Ninin. I'll just finish filling this out and be on my way."

"Relax," Captain Lotuk said. "You can see him right now — how would that be?"

"Are you detaining me?" I whispered.

"Captain!" the officer at the high desk exclaimed, clearly eager to offer his opinion on the topic, but Captain Lotuk raised a long-fingered hand, and he said not another word. She hadn't turned her attention from me the whole time, and now, without answering my question, she beckoned me through the door and into the interior of Civil Order's West Ward offices.

We walked down a narrow corridor with numbered doors on either side, then took a lift down a floor, maybe several floors, exited, turned a corner — and then Captain Lotuk was opening a door to a small office very much like Decommissioner Five's, with binders lining shelves along a side wall and a desk supporting a database access console and piles of folders and loose papers.

"Have a seat," the captain said, indicating a chair on one side of the desk and making her way to the other side. Seemingly out of nowhere she drew a pitcher of water and lemon slices, along with a cup. She filled it and passed it to me. It was a relief to drink — cool and refreshing. When I set the cup down it was empty.

"I'm not detaining you," she said. "But I thought we'd have a brief chat before I let you see Mr. Ninin."

I nodded. She had the same air of authority as Five, but she was taller and longer limbed. And like the officer in the reception hall, her hair was no more than a fine dark fuzz following the contours of her skull.

"You really seem to have made something of your life," Captain Lotuk said, her eyes traveling to my Ministry badge.

"I… Thank you."

"Children of parents like yours generally come to no good," she said. "But you're the exception."

What could I say to that? I lowered my eyes, focused on the droplets of water condensing on the pitcher, now out of reach on the other side of the desk.

"Would you say you're a happy person? A loyal citizen of the Polity?"

"Yes!" I said, looking up.

Captain Lotuk's brow wrinkled. "So why have you suddenly decided to befriend an undesirable like Mr. Ninin? Someone like you, I'd think the last thing you'd want to do is jeopardize the life you've made for yourself, against all odds."

"He's not an undesirable! I-I mean, he's, he's—" *He's a teacher,* I wanted to say. *He's helping people out in the workforce broaden their horizons. He's curious; he cares about the truth.* But then there was the fact that he had sneaked back onto Daybreak Ventures' property after being banned, that he'd removed artifacts without permission. To save them, to be sure, but in Captain Lotuk's eyes it would still be theft. It was still theft.

"He's a retrogressivist and a vandal who caused significant damage to a major development project. It's only luck that no one was hurt," Captain Lotuk supplied, when I didn't finish my sentence.

"He didn't do it, and you know it!" The words were out of my mouth before I could stop them, and now my heart leapt up to follow. What had I done? I crossed my arms against my stomach, bracing myself.

"I don't know that at all," Captain Lotuk said mildly. "Are you suggesting someone else placed explosives there?"

"I just mean—if explosives were used, then why was the Ministry of Divinities contacted? Why were we asked to look into it?"

"There does seem to have been some bureaucratic miscommunication there," Captain Lotuk acknowledged.

I highly doubted it was a matter of miscommunication. If explosives had truly been involved, there would have been no reason whatsoever to contact the Ministry of Divinities. But the Ministry had been contacted. The story of explosives had come later. But why?

If Captain Lotuk was going to insist that explosives had caused the damage, I couldn't contradict her. She was watching me expectantly.

"Whatever happened, Mr. Ninin couldn't have had anything to do with it. He didn't even know about it—he was horrified when I mentioned it," I said at last.

"Do you have any other candidates for the culprit?" she asked—pleasantly, as if she were asking for dessert suggestions for a commemorative banquet. And then, in the same tone, "Are *you* involved, Ms. Manu? Are you maybe the instigator? Some kind of long-game revenge for a perceived injustice?"

I felt it like a physical blow.

"No! No, of course not! I was *assigned* this case, I—"

Captain Lotuk interrupted me, her brow wrinkled again. "Am I recalling correctly that you were assigned because of concern that a decommissioned god might be involved? One you decommissioned? But you botched the job, somehow? And by interesting coincidence, he was one of the deities worshiped by the population subject to the Sweet Harbor Relocation Initiative, some decades back? People were willing to massacre innocents over that, back in the day, as you're aware—I apologize for touching on a painful topic."

An overwhelming nausea gripped me.

"I need a bathroom," I choked out.

"Of course, of course. I'll take you. But do answer me first: are you involved?"

"No!" And then I retched. Fortunately, I hadn't eaten anything that day, or the papers on Captain Lotuk's desk would have suffered. She appeared unruffled.

"There, there," she said, stepping to my side and helping me stand. "Let's get you to the bathroom. We'll talk again another time." Then, into her unicom, "Have Mr. Ninin brought to C4."

She led me to a bathroom, where I rinsed out my mouth, splashed my face, and retwisted and fastened my hair. She smiled blandly when I came out. We continued down a corridor to a cluster of doors. An officer stood sentry by one. As Captain Lotuk approached, he opened it. She stepped aside, but I hung back.

"Go on," she said, as if to a small child. I stepped in.

It was a tiny box of a room, completely empty except for three stools, two in the center of the room and one in the corner right by the door. Ateni, dressed in gruel-colored prisoners' garb and with his hands restrained, sat hunched up on one. At the sight of me, his eyes widened.

"Have a seat." Captain Lotuk indicated the stool next to his. She settled herself on the stool by the door.

"You're staying in the room?" I asked.

"Yes." Another bland smile.

I climbed onto the stool next to Ateni.

"What's going on?" he asked, in a low voice that wasn't quite a whisper. "Why are you here?"

"It's strange, isn't it," Captain Lotuk put in from her perch in the corner. "A complete stranger until yesterday, and yet she's visiting you here! Few lifelong friends would be that devoted."

Ateni scowled at her, and the frown remained when he turned back to me.

I cleared my throat. "I just wanted to tell you that you were right," I began. I licked my lips, swallowed. "About the knots, the Laloran-morna knots. They are from before. The other Sweet Harbor gods confirmed it. Your theory was correct. And there's more—there was a garden, and…"

For a moment Ateni straightened and his eyes lit up, but the brightness faded as quickly as a struck match.

"That's good to know," he said. Then, bitterly, "Maybe I can write a paper—a decade or half-decade from now, when I'm done with rehabilitation and reeducation."

"Don't talk that way," I said. "If the real cause of the flooding comes to light, they'll release you. And it will come to light." There was so much more I wanted to say, but not with Captain Lotuk sitting right there. For a brief moment I wondered about that. Why was she in the room with us? Surely all visits were audiovisually recorded anyway—why be physically present?

Ateni was shaking his head. "They have it in for me. Because of a box of fireworks at my apartment."

"Fireworks?" I echoed, confused. "Like for—"

"Like for First Harvest Festival," he said, an edge to his voice. He squeezed his eyes shut, opened them, blinked. I realized that not only were his hands restrained, but that the restraint was fastened at his waist. If his eyes were itching or hurting, he couldn't rub them.

"Are those the explosives you're talking about?" I demanded, swiveling round to face Captain Lotuk. "Are you saying Daybreak Ventures was attacked with fireworks?"

"It's a known retrogressivist method: disassemble fireworks and use the powder to create a larger device."

"Lots of people have fireworks," I said. Before I'd been sweating; now I was beginning to shiver. "If you were going to detain everyone who has fireworks—"

"Yes, lots of people have fireworks, and they keep track of where they purchase them, as required by law. But Mr. Ninin here can't recall where he bought his. Now maybe that's because they're not really his. Perhaps he's holding them for a friend, and that's the person I should be asking for a sales record. But Mr. Ninin says no, the fireworks are his own. And yet"—she shrugged—"he doesn't have a sales record and can't recall where he bought them!"

I looked to Ateni for some sign of what all this meant, but he was staring fixedly at the floor near the base of my stool.

"Perhaps now you realize, Ms. Manu, that an afternoon's acquaintance isn't really enough for an assessment of a person's character," Captain Lotuk observed, and then, addressing Ateni, she said, "But you're as much misled as misleading, Mr. Ninin. You never even learned the name of your surprising advocate, did you. Ninin Ateni, meet Manu Sae, born Jowa Sae. She's the daughter of Jowa Fen and Manu Nakra, the Fifteen Breezes Relocation Center bombers. Her parents killed your parents."

At this Ateni looked up, shock and disbelief overspreading his face, his eyes seeking mine.

"It's the truth; she won't deny it," Captain Lotuk told him gently. Then she hopped down from her stool and clapped her hands, whereupon the officer outside opened the door. "We're finished for today," she said. "Think on what I told you earlier, Mr. Ninin. Contrition and confession are good for the spirit. Ms. Manu, come with me. Officer, please take Mr. Ninin back to holding."

"Why did you tell him that?" I cried, trotting to keep up with Captain Lotuk's quick strides. I tried to catch a last glimpse of Ateni over my shoulder, but the muscular form of the Civil Order officer blocked all but the back of his head from view.

"Doesn't he deserve to know?" returned Captain Lotuk. "You're asking him to trust you, making him promises, and you haven't even told him your name! He'll be much better off if he takes responsibility for the Daybreak Ventures incident and gets rehabilitated."

"But he didn't do it!"

"You still don't think so? Even though you know he was keeping explosives at his apartment? Think about it for a moment."

I did. Was it possible that the Ministry really had been contacted in error, and explosives really had been used? And could Ateni—who, as the captain pointed out, I didn't really know anything about—have planted them? Could he have been feigning horror when I told him about the flooding? And was the story of Laloran-morna and Goblet unrelated to the incident?

Captain Lotuk smiled into my silence. "Thank you for coming in, Ms. Manu." She opened the door to the reception hall, but I didn't move.

"If I find the real culprit, will you let Mr. Ninin go?" I asked.

Her smile deepened, but she said nothing.

"If he didn't do it, you'd have no reason to keep him, right?" I pressed, and when she still didn't respond, I added, "It's heterodox to detain the innocent."

Captain Lotuk's smile evaporated. "Everyone is guilty of something. If you give me the least grounds, I'll have you brought back here. So watch yourself. Goodbye now." With a light but firm touch, she propelled me through the door and shut it.

I was aware of heads turning as I made my way past the ranks of benches, and as I reached the entrance doors, I realized several people were following me.

There was the elderly crossing guard and a man in a gardener's smock who stood proprietorially close to her. There was a young woman in a sanitary worker's coveralls, and a pale-skinned, middle-aged man whose right arm hung unresponsively at his side.

"Did you see Professor Ninin?" the crossing guard asked, palms pressed together in supplication. "Is he all right? We're so worried about him."

"He w-would never do anything w-wrong," the middle-aged man said. "It's g-got to be some kind of..." his mouth twisted for a moment "m-mistake."

"He's the best teacher I ever had," declared the sanitary worker.

"I did. I did see him," I said. Their anxious faces wrung my heart. "He's..." It was no good; I couldn't lie about his situation or state of mind, so I changed direction. "He's lucky to have such devoted students. Having people stand by you at times like this helps."

"We all got summoned for questioning," the sanitary worker said, scowling. "But they haven't even called us yet. It's taking forever — we're going to lose a whole day's pay."

"And they won't tell us anything," the crossing guard said. Then, hopefully, "Are you an advocate?"

"No Kavia," said the gardener. "Don't you see the badge? That's Ministry of Divinities."

The crossing guard's face fell. "Oh! Oh yes, I see. I beg your pardon."

"That's quite all right. I want to help Mr. Ninin — Professor Ninin — if I can."

"Osh Kavia!" barked the officer at the front of the reception hall.

"That's me!" said the crossing guard, wide-eyed. "It's my turn."

"We'll go up together," said the gardener, slipping his arm through hers."

"T-Tren's come out," said the middle-aged man, pointing with his good hand to the door I'd come through moments earlier. The little group returned to the front of the hall, the gardener escorting the crossing guard to the high desk and the other two heading for their classmate.

I pushed the heavy front doors open. The scent of steaming asphalt and vehicle emissions greeted me, with other odors threading through the humid air — tobacco, garbage, perfume. There must have been a cloudburst while I'd been inside: the gutters hemming the streets were tiny rushing rivers, and the vehicles' wheels hissed over the sheen of water that couldn't be channeled away.

I checked my unicom and found a message from Ms. Bama. Laloran-morna was back at home. I did some quick mental calculations, then sent her a message saying to expect company and approximately when. Then I sent a message to Nakona, the only one of the retired Sweet Harbor gods who has the knack for using a unicom. "Can you reserve a boat for moon-viewing tonight?" I recorded. "For Lolo. Send the others to fetch him. His Compassionate Care attendant will help you."

What about you? Aren't you coming? she sent back. It pained me not to answer, but I couldn't. Instead, I headed briskly for the nearest stop where I could catch a bus back to the Ministry — and quickly became aware of the slap of rubber sandals on wet pavement behind me, faster when I picked up my pace, slower when I slackened.

I wheeled round and found myself face-to-face with a weedy, sullen-faced man, maybe in his late twenties, in threadbare trousers with frayed cuffs, wearing an unbuttoned shirt like a jacket and nothing else up top.

"What do you want?" I asked, as aggressively and haughtily as I could manage.

The man took a step back, and for a moment I thought he might run. Instead he narrowed his eyes and thrust his skinny chest forward. "You talked to the Civies," he said. "You wanted to see Ateni—and they let you."

"What business is that of yours?

"He's my foster brother. Always looked after me." The man glowered, then muttered, "He's in trouble because of me."

I crossed my arms. "Let me guess. The fireworks in his apartment are yours."

"Yeah, but I swear they're legit! I have the sales papers! I was going to rent a cart, sell festival stuff, you know? Toys and decorations and fireworks, all that stuff—but the rental fell through. I didn't make a bomb!" He glanced back toward Civil Order's offices.

"Neither did Ateni," I said, "but your fireworks in his apartment aren't helping his case any. You should bring in the papers—at least it would clear up that part of his charge."

"No way. I already had my chat with them, but I didn't tell them nothing. 'I don't know, I don't know, I don't know.' That's the only tune I'm singing."

"So you're fine with Ateni going through rehabilitation and reeducation because of your fireworks?"

"No, I'm not fine with it! But if I tell them the fireworks are mine, they'll just take me in too."

"But you said they were legitimate! You have papers!"

The man's lip curled scornfully. "Like that's ever stopped the Civies from detaining someone. If they decide they want to get you, they get you, one way — or another. Would've thought you'd know that."

"What's that supposed to mean?"

He stared at me incredulously and I glared back. People flowed around us on the sidewalk, unaware.

"The Civie at the main desk called you Jowa," he said in a low voice.

My heart banged against my ribs.

"That was a mistake. My name is Manu. Manu Sae."

The man's eyes widened. "Then it's true," he whispered. "You're Jowa Fen and Manu Nakra's daughter."

I turned and walked away, fast, but the man came after me, his hand closing on my arm like a metal band.

"Let. Me. Go," I said, trying to keep the quaver out of my voice. But he didn't let go.

"Say it's true!" he urged — and if he was trying to keep his voice steady, he was as unsuccessful as I'd been.

"It means *nothing!* I'm *nothing* like them," I said, with such vehemence that passersby shot us concerned glances.

"Some people think they're heroes."

I couldn't believe my ears.

"They killed 214 people," I said. "They were murderers."

Thirty-two years ago the Polity's Central Planning Committee approved a project to modernize and redevelop the Sweet Harbor District. Old higgledy-piggledy neighborhoods—houses, workplaces, schools, markets, and shrines—were razed, and the population placed in relocation centers to await the completion of the promised new neighborhoods. The relocation centers were austere places administered by Civil Order, and the wait wasn't a short one. One year stretched into two, and people grew restless, but no one was permitted to move elsewhere unless they had either the promise of work or family to act as a guarantor in the destination location—requirements almost no one could meet. Those whose livelihoods had not been disrupted by the construction were free to leave for work during daylight hours, but at night everyone had to be present and accounted for, and the relocation center gates were locked. Everyone else had to remain behind those gates, day in and day out.

Eventually there were demonstrations, especially at the Fifteen Breezes Relocation Center, which was in a low-lying area that flooded every time it rained. Civil Order's oversight became more stringent in response.

As the second year of confinement in the relocation centers drew to a close, there were those—especially, tragically, in Fifteen Breezes—who turned to more violent means of seeking redress. On an evening when a huge cyclone was scheduled to make landfall and Civil Order's forces were largely preoccupied overseeing evacuations, two extremists in the Fifteen Breezes Relocation Center forced their way into the Civil Order administrative barracks attached to the center and laid explosives, which detonated early, killing one of the extremists and three Civil Order officers. Worse, the rubble from the explosion blocked Fifteen Breezes' entrance gate—the only way in or out. When the cyclone hit, terrified residents found themselves trapped between a powerful storm surge and massive pieces of broken concrete. Two hundred eleven died—either drowned or trampled. The surviving extremist was condemned and executed.

Those were my parents.

"They were murderers," I repeated. "They left me an orphan—me and others. They weren't heroes."

A memory: the odor of cooking oil and also, faintly, jasmine—my grandmother's scent. The softness of her well-worn blouse against my cheek as I buried my face in her chest and lost myself in tears, surrounded by that scent and her arms.

I came back to the present. My eyes were dry. The young man had finally released my arm, and now was simply staring at me, almost solemnly, with no sneer.

"I guess that's the way your fosters would've told it," he said.

"My *grandparents.*"

"Your grandparents raised you? Oh, well definitely then. Kind of surprised they were able to keep custody of you, to be honest. Bet Civil Order made them report every living thing about you. Bet you had to be just perfect."

Another memory: my grandfather drilling me in Thought Orthodoxy maxims. *You have to get this right.* His face so stern, so severe.

"It didn't really happen the way we learn in school," the man said.

"Like you would know," I said. "You weren't even born then." I was pretty sure of this — I'd been only five, and this man was several years younger than I was.

"People who lived through it told me. My big sister. Ateni's aunt and uncle. Other people."

"I'm not interested," I said, but I made no move to go. He gave me a long look.

"There'd been protests —"

"I know that," I cut in.

"So the place was on lockdown," he continued, slowly, dropping his head, so I couldn't see his expression. "The Civies should've been evacuating everyone—there was a big storm coming—but they said they wouldn't unlock the gates until the protest organizers came forward."

An awful, choking sensation was rising within me, a filthy turbid feeling.

"It was a standoff. The wind was already up and the rain had started. Your parents were committed to the protest movement, and somehow they'd managed to lay hands on demolition explosives. They were going to blow up the gates so everyone could get out."

"But their plan backfired. The wreckage trapped everyone, and more than 200 people died," I whispered.

"No! People could've walked right through. It was the Civies. They started firing on people as they came out! People were caught between gunfire and floodwaters. Survivors said you knew your relative had been shot if they said the body wasn't recovered. 'Wasn't recovered' meant it had bullets in it."

I clapped my hands to my ears. "Shut up! Just shut up! I don't want to hear any more."

"Daughter, can I help you?"

I jerked away from a touch on my shoulder and found myself face to face with an elderly gentleman in monastic robes. My throat ached.

"I'm fine," I muttered, casting a quick look around, but there were no lingering spectators and, thankfully, no sign of anyone from Civil Order.

"Are you sure? Is this man harassing you?"

The young man was still there, hands jammed into the pockets of his trousers, expression surly but remote.

"No. I apologize for the disturbance. It was bad news. I wasn't prepared."

"If you're sure..." He glanced doubtfully at my unwelcome companion. When neither of us said anything more, the monk lifted his hand. "Then peace to you, daughter. Son." He nodded to us, and the sun winked off badges for the Abstractions of Compassion, Reason, and Community on his sash. In a few seconds he was just another figure in the crowd.

"I'm going back to the Ministry," I said unsteadily.

"You don't believe me."

"Believe that Civil Order massacred Polity citizens during a cyclone? No." The choking feeling was rising again. I started walking. The bus stop. The Ministry. Laloran-morna. There were things I had to do.

The man followed a few steps behind. "There's proof. If you go to the archives of *City News* or any of the other dailies and—"

"I'm not going to do that," I said through clenched teeth, without looking back. I picked up my speed. "I have better ways to spend my time."

"You know, you're right!" he shouted after me, "you're nothing like your parents!" The words were heavy with contempt.

Righteous retorts and blistering counter-insults sprang to mind and died without reaching my tongue. I was running now and didn't stop, even when the bus stop came into sight. I just kept going, spurred by feelings I had no name for, feelings so deep and powerful they threatened to tear me apart from the inside. At last I ducked into a public toilet, and in that rank, stifling space I gave way to deep, silent sobs. And then, emptied, I wiped my eyes, adjusted my clothes, stepped out, and hailed a courtesy vehicle.

Civil Order was intimidating, high-handed, opaque, but was it—? Could it—? As the courtesy vehicle wove through traffic, the question presented itself for my consideration over and over again, and over and over again I shied away from it.

My grandparents must have known the truth— whatever it was. The shame and sorrow etched permanently in their faces—what if the cause wasn't their daughter's crime, as I'd always imagined? What if it was their own participation in her defamation?

No.

But each time I pushed the idea away, it slithered back.

"We've arrived, ma'am."

I paid the driver and went to the conference room where Tailin and Feshi were still working.

"What happened? You look like you were hit by a truck!" Tailin exclaimed.

Feshi stifled a giggle. "That's not a thing you should say to someone," she told him. To me she said, "You never got that tea Tailin requested for you — I'll get you a fresh one."

"Seriously, though," Tailin said, when we were alone. "Did it go so badly with Laloran-morna?"

"I couldn't speak with him — he had a health crisis," I said, barricading and sandbagging away the feelings surging inside me.

"I'm sorry." Tailin said, with genuine sympathy. "I know you're close."

"I spoke with the other retired Sweet Harbor gods, though, asked some questions, but—" I swallowed. Everything from here forward was going to require deception, and I hate deception.

"But?"

"I— I don't think it's worth pursuing any further."

He nodded slowly.

"That's hard too. You seemed very committed to your theory."

New tears were threatening. I blinked them away. "That's how it goes, though, doesn't it," I said. "One minute you're sure of something; next minute—" I forced a smile, shrugged. "Everything's different."

Tailin's brow creased. "Is there something else going on?"

I shook my head, not trusting myself to speak.

Tailin's frown deepened. "Do you still feel up to seeing the exhibition tonight? Maybe you'd rather go home and get to sleep early?"

"No! I want to go to the exhibition!" I said, maybe a little too forcefully. Seeing the surprise on Tailin's face, I added, "It'll take my mind off things."

Feshi returned with a tea tray before Tailin could say or ask anything more. Her face was grave.

"Five came into the kitchen while the tea was brewing," she said. "She wants to see you. Here. You may as well fortify yourself." She poured a cup and handed it to me. It was the smoky stuff the Ministry buys in bulk. Just a few sips of it—aromatic, bitter—soothed me. That was enough. I set it down and headed for Five's office.

Why had Captain Lotuk's office reminded me of Five's? Experiencing them in this order, I could only think of the differences—Five's office had a window, for one, even if it was a narrow one, and there was a photo of her spouse and children on her desk, and all manner of representations of various deities, active and decommissioned, not to mention Abstractions, on shelves and walls.

"Ma'am. You asked to see me?"

Five looked up. Maybe that was it: maybe it was the authority of the person occupying the space, and my own smallness.

"I was speaking with that captain from Civil Order just now," she said. "That's twice today. I prefer to keep my interactions with Civil Order to zero. Oh for goodness sake don't hover on the threshold like a ghost; come in. Sit."

I complied.

"She said you wanted to see the detainee in the Daybreak Ventures case."

Five didn't wait for me to confirm this. She had told me to sit, but she herself stood and began to pace, back stiff, shoulders tight.

"She wanted to know if I had authorized the visit. She asked about my *sympathies*." There was a tremble in her voice at that last word. Fear? Anger? Probably both. A bright bar of late afternoon sunlight bisected her face as she paused by the window.

"You had a specific task today," she said. "What were you doing out in the city?"

"I was following up on something related to the undecommissioned goddess...but nothing came of it. Going to Civil Order wasn't part of that."

"Going to Civil Order shouldn't be part of anything! You told me you only met that man yesterday. What business could you possibly have had trying to see him?"

"I just— I happened to find out something related to his research, and I thought... I know he has more serious things to worry about, but it can feel good to know that—"

Five interrupted me with a half-disbelieving, half-resigned laugh. "If anyone else were to tell me they visited a new acquaintance in detention purely to pass along a research note, I would be offended by the clumsy attempt at a lie, but from you? It seems only too likely to be true." She sighed. "Would it be fair, then, to say that you used work time to take care of a personal matter?"

I took a deep breath. Using work time for personal matters was an infraction—but nothing like linking Ministry work to a purported crime.

"Yes," I said.

Five's shoulders relaxed, and she slipped back into her seat. She opened a drawer and pulled out a form.

"Then I'm going to have to reprimand you," she said. "And"—this next more to herself than to me—"I'll let Captain Lotuk know I've done that, so she understands I'm taking the situation seriously. I did warn you." I thought I could hear regret in her voice. "I gave you a direct order, which you ignored. I'm not writing you up for that, but I can't protect you from the consequences. My primary responsibility is to the Ministry's work."

"Yes, ma'am. I understand that."

She softened. "I was surprised and pleased to hear about the goddess you and the others uncovered. She's rather peripheral to Sweet Harbor, but still—that's good work."

But she's not the one, I thought.

"Thank you," I said. "It was Thirty-Six who found her."

"With your guidance," Five said.

"It was a team effort."

Five smiled. "Just so. All right, I won't keep you any longer. Don't worry too much about the reprimand; everyone gets caught doing personal business now and then. But Thirty-Seven."

"Yes, ma'am?"

"It might not be a bad idea to incorporate a prayer to Prudence into your daily ritual, if it's not part of it already, and if it is, then add another."

"Yes, ma'am."

She wouldn't like my plans for the evening, but there was no helping that. Five, Tailin, my grandparents... There were so many people, living and dead, whom I might fail tonight. The one person I absolutely could not fail was Laloran-morna. Captain Lotuk was right: I had botched his decommissioning. But I could make sure he left his mortal life in peace. And maybe doing so would prevent future flooding where Lotus Estuary used to be and bring some justice for Ateni.

Back at the conference room, Tailin and Feshi were finishing up. They closed in on either side of me as I entered.

"Was it terrible?" Tailin asked. "Five was asking earlier today why you'd gone out—she definitely wasn't happy."

"She was furious," murmured Feshi.

"It'll be all right," I said. I highly doubted that, but it was the response that left the least room for further questions, especially when I didn't volunteer anything more. Sure enough, the other two didn't press me. Instead, Tailin had me look over the finished list of references for the search terms I'd suggested, and Feshi showed me the brief she'd created on the goddess of the northern current.

"Tailin says the two of you are going to the Art of the Abstractions exhibition this evening," Feshi ventured presently. "Would it be all right if I tagged along? And then maybe we could all get something to eat together?"

A spike of panic shot through me. I hadn't foreseen this complication, and yet what could I say? To object would be to suggest I was treating the date as something more than an arrangement between companionable friends, and I certainly didn't want to do that. What I was planning was already too big a trespass on my friendship with Tailin.

And then it hit me that having Feshi along might actually solve a problem.

"That's an excellent idea," I said. My enthusiasm sounded false in my own ears, but Feshi grinned.

Tailin seemed momentarily startled at my easy agreement, and for a half-second I wondered if he was disappointed. But surely not. Now he was nodding approvingly. We agreed to go home to change and to reconvene at the exhibition.

Alone, I considered how much time I had. My eyes drifted to my unicom. *No,* I reminded myself. Any communication could be monitored and the device itself tracked. Ateni had been the one who pointed that out to me. Ateni, who was looking at years of rehabilitation and reeducation... I gritted my teeth: *focus!*

My instinct, once I reached my apartment, was to rush, but I made myself sit down and think carefully about next steps. Kadiuk's protests notwithstanding, Goblet was a tutelary deity. How much could I remember about decommissioning a tutelary deity without accessing the Ministry's databases? The primary requirement was to be in the place associated with the deity, but of course that was impossible. But with the knot stones Ateni had hidden on the mangrove spit, it ought to be possible to create a simulacrum of Cup of the Sea. I closed my eyes, recalling everything Laloran-morna and Kadiuk had said, describing the place. A garden of ruby slenderweed and jade mussels. I'd have to stop by a market—but I couldn't do that before going to the exhibition. I suppressed a shaky giggle at the thought of walking past sculptures, paintings, and votary items with a bag full of seaweed and shellfish.

I took some beads of divine resin out of my decommissioner's satchel and slipped them into a pretty, long-strapped bag that my grandmother had given me when I graduated from university. Then I looked around for an envelope. On my kitchen counter, in a pile of bills and solicitations, was an envelope from the apartment manager containing a notice about an inspection of the building's fire prevention systems later in the week. I left the notice on the counter, unclasped my unicom, slipped it off my wrist, and put it in the envelope. Then I pressed the envelope closed again and put it in my bag on top of the beads of divine resin.

Next I changed out of my work clothes. Since I don't socialize, I don't have much of a leisure wardrobe: the short-sleeved silk shirt in cheerful yellow that I chose was the same vintage as the bag with the long strap, and like the bag had been a present from my grandmother. It had a wrap that went with it, patterned with plumeria blossoms, but that seemed too dressy (and hard to move about in quickly). I ended up putting my black work trousers back on. I left my Ministry badge by my grandparents' memorial photo and tried to block out the sense of finality the gesture gave me. It was ridiculous; I take off the badge every night.

One more deep breath, and I was ready to go out.

The Art of the Abstractions exhibition was in the city center in the new Museum of Arts and Culture, a modernist structure intended to call to mind a fish leaping from the water, but which looked to me more like a paper sack that had been twisted in the middle—if you imagine a paper sack clad in white marble. The lights illuminating its façade transitioned slowly through the spectrum, blue to purple to red to orange and so on. It was crowded inside, but Feshi, looking stylish in a short magenta dress with a gold ribbon braided through her hair, found me right away and caught me by the arm. Tailin was beside her, dressed in a featherweight indigo jacket and wrap patterned with ferns and incense cones, white on indigo.

"Welcome! I only just got here myself—Tailin beat both of us," Feshi exclaimed. "You've got to see the representation of Music they have right in the center—it's an inland lute, only giant sized. I wonder if it's really playable."

"Instruments seem to be the theme for the Abstraction of Music," Tailin said. "I guess that's not surprising. See the coconut drums from Kis Province? And over there are some double pipes from the Northwest."

"But look, there's Majihina," I said, pointing to a tiny ebony statue of an old man with a child's face who held a shallow bowl in his hands. "I always think of him more as a god of insight and wisdom than of music — isn't he listed as an expression of Wisdom on the official roster?"

"He is," Tailin agreed. He peered at the description accompanying the statue. "It says that the artist was thinking about the insights that come through music." He looked up, thoughtful. "That's an interesting blending of Abstractions."

"Music does bring powerful insights — or maybe intuitions," Feshi said.

"I'm just glad to see Majihina's face," I said, resisting the urge to stroke the statue's cheek. We were all silent after that, because mention of actual deities in the context of Abstractions always brings up questions about what will happen to the Department of Decommissioning once the transition to worship of Abstractions is complete. Some say it never will be, because folk deities keep arising, and of course there's always the possibility that the shift to Abstractions will be one day be reversed. But if things continue as they are now, at best the department will be much reduced—Abstractions don't require decommissioning in the same way instantiated deities do.

Without my unicom on, I had no way of checking the time, but I had planned on only ten or so minutes of actual attendance at the exhibition. I needed to lay the groundwork for my departure.

"Speaking of seeing faces," I said, "I'm afraid I won't be able to stay very long after all, because I need to check in with Laloran-morna. I got word that he's back at his apartment... He may not live much longer... I have to see him."

"Of course," said Tailin.

Feshi added hesitantly, "If you think your visit won't be very long, maybe you could still catch us at the restaurant after. I was thinking of the new place a block from here. It's called Zodiac—they claim each day's special is created in alignment with the season, phase of the moon, ascendant stars and planets, all that kind of thing. Just in fun, of course—they've got a disclaimer about not promoting superstitions and so on and so on... Any chance you could make it, do you think?"

Her face was hopeful. How had I missed the friendliness in Feshi until today?

"I doubt it," I said, my regret genuine. "But I'd like to try it some other time."

Feshi nodded. "I'm sorry about Laloran-morna. Tailin told me about your friendship with him." She glanced down at the little statue of Majihina. "You're lucky. I've never stayed friends with any deity I decommissioned — not that I've decommissioned very many, yet. Mainly I've helped out on bigger jobs. I was part of the team that decommissioned Nafa." She grimaced. "Did you hear about that case? Up in Heaven's Teeth?"

Tailin frowned. "The one that was mixed up with the Deep Ore Mines disturbances? That was a tough one."

I remembered the case. Historically, Nafa had been a deity of darkness and the depths, a god to be feared and propitiated, but he had evolved, during years of dissatisfaction over wages and conditions at Deep Ore Mines, into either a champion of the miners (if you spoke to the miners) or a god of extortion (if you listened to the complaints of the mine administrators).

"It really was," Feshi said fervently. "There was a lot of negotiation, and eventually it was agreed that the dispute between the miners and the administrators would go to extra-regional arbitration, and Nafa would be commemorated as an expression of Justice. But the god still fought the decommissioning, and afterward he boasted that he'd be redeified in no time, due to local regard."

"And did that happen?" I asked. I recalled hearing about the official outcome of the case, but not any follow-up.

"No... I think there was a lot of monitoring of the population immediately following the decommissioning, to—well, you know, to prevent that. And then the extra-regional arbitration did end up satisfying a lot of demands." Her lips pinched in a sour grin. "And I heard from one of the more senior decommissioners that the Abstraction of Justice is very, very popular there now."

"Not all decommissionings are good ones," Tailin said sympathetically, "but it sounds like all in all things ended well."

"Oh, for sure," Feshi said quickly. "I don't mean to complain. And the two solo cases I've had have been no problem. I just never— It just must be interesting to have one you stay in touch with."

"It is," I said. Too many thoughts, all of them unsharable, crowded my mind. I licked my lips. "I really wish things were different. This was— This was a pleasure, even just these few minutes." My hand trembled as I reached into my bag for the envelope with my unicom in it. I held it out to Tailin. "Would you be willing to drop this by my apartment building on your way home? Just leave it with the building manager? I-I intended to leave it at the manager's office on my way out, but I was so distracted, I forgot—and I'm late with it; really I should have had it in yesterday, but—and I think you're likely to be heading home before I am—the office closes at the twenty-first hour—and if—"

"It's fine; it's fine!" Tailin said, laughing a little. He took it from me and tucked it away in an inner pocket of his jacket.

"Thank you. I'm very sorry for the inconvenience, and for—"

"It's not an inconvenience. Relax, Thirty-Seven. Sae. It's fine," he said.

"—everything," I finished, but it was lost in his reassurance. I bowed my head to each of them, then hurried off on legs that felt like water.

Yes, it was good that Feshi was there. If she hadn't joined us, Tailin might have simply given up on the exhibition, once I said I had to leave. But with Feshi eager to see it, he—and my unicom—would continue the evening as planned. If Civil Order was monitoring my location, then it would appear I was still at the exhibition, just as I'd made it known publicly that I'd be. Anyone tracking the unicom would see that I went out for an evening meal at Zodiac and then made my way back to my apartment building. Tailin would leave the envelope with the office manager, who, I sincerely hoped, would then slip it through my mail slot, thereby conveying "me" the rest of the way home. There were ways this plan could go wrong, but whatever happened, the report from my unicom would be that I was nowhere near Daybreak Ventures' development site.

Without my unicom or Ministry badge, I felt unmoored, all ties to normal life cut, and in the yellow silk shirt, with the little bag slung across me, it was as if I'd exchanged my body—and life—for someone else's. Someone without a dreadful past, someone with no entanglements with Civil Order, no troubles at work. In this untethered state, I stopped by a fishmonger's stall and picked up an order of jade mussels—only just in time: they were packing up for the night.

"We don't have any fresh slenderweed," the man told me as he placed refrigerator packs on top of his last cooler of fish and latched the lid closed. "You can get it dried at any grocery, though." Reluctantly, I made a detour to the nearest grocery, then hurried on to Sweet Harbor Community Apartments West Branch, Building 2.

A distressed Ms. Bama welcomed me in. From the threshold I could hear Anin, Malirin, and Kadiuk talking animatedly, and when I stepped in, I could see them gathered at the entrance to Laloran-morna's sleeping quarters.

"You didn't respond to any of my messages!" Ms. Bama said. "They're saying they're taking the holy one to the sea, but he's only just back from hospital—he's much too weak! He might—I don't know how much more time he has."

Her lips trembled, and I noticed the bags under her eyes. It had surely been a long, hard day for her.

"It's important to him to get to the sea before his final moment comes," I said. "It's his last wish. You remember yesterday — he asked about his love? We have to try to let him see her."

Ms. Bama's eyes widened when I mentioned Goblet. "Oh yes...yes," she said, nodding, but then, leaning in close to me, she said quietly, "It's just, I don't know how we can manage it."

"We'll help you, child," said Kadiuk, as if he'd been listening all along. "Now that Sweeting's here, there are four of us — five if you'll come."

"Of course I will," Ms. Bama said, pulling herself up tall, though she's a tiny woman. "But you don't understand; you can't just put him on your back or..."

While we had been talking, Anin and Malirin had somehow managed to remove the sheets from Laloran-morna's hospital bed and had tied them into a sort of sling that hung between the two of them. Leaning back on his rush mat in this sling was Laloran-morna, eyes half closed.

"Can you switch this to the portable one?" he whispered, tapping the plastic tubing connecting him to the bedside oxygen concentrator. Without a word, Ms. Bama expertly connected the tubes to a portable pack and set it beside him in the sling.

"Ready?" Anin asked Malirin, who smiled by way of answer. In unison they stepped forward.

"Good," murmured Laloran-morna, barely audible. "I've got a promise to keep."

Me too, I thought.

"Do we know when we'll be back?" Ms. Bama asked, twisting her clasped hands uneasily. "I need to send a message to Mr. Teka. He has the night shift again today."

"Tell him you had to take Laloran-morna back to hospital," I said. "Say you're staying there with him and that Mr. Teka doesn't need to do his shift today."

She frowned. "Lie to him?"

It's one thing to decide to lie, myself; it's another thing to ask someone else to.

"If you try to explain what's really happening," I said slowly, "he'll be confused and concerned. He'll probably contact Compassionate Care to ask about protocols, and they may not see the value in what we're doing. They'll probably only see the risk."

"I'm sure that's all they'll see," Ms. Bama said.

"Sweeting!" called Kadiuk from the hallway. "What's keeping you?"

"Ride the lift on down," I called back. "We'll—I'll— meet you downstairs." Then to Ms. Bama, "I don't want you to do this if you don't want to. You can stay here and explain that we did it against your will and your recommendation."

Ms. Bama looked toward the empty hospital bed, then turned back to me, her face serious. "Every patient is different. This would be wrong for many...but it's right for the holy one. And I don't want anything to interrupt it. I'll tell Mr. Teka we had to return to hospital." She recorded and sent the message, and we hurried after the others.

We were too many to fit into one courtesy vehicle, and Ms. Bama insisted on riding in the one that carried Laloran-morna—all for the best, as she was able to call on the authority of her position as a Compassionate Care attendant to insist there was nothing untoward about conveying him to Fairest Moonlight Electraboat Rentals, where Nakona and a very skeptical manager waited for us.

"I was telling your friend," the man said, when we'd all assembled by the counter, "this isn't a good evening for moon viewing. The moon isn't even going to rise until half past the twenty-second hour, and we close at midnight—unless you want to do an overnight rental, but then you have to keep it until we open at the ninth hour, and there's no discount for that. And with the rains...and tomorrow's a workday..."

"We'll have the boat back to you by midnight," I assured him.

With a sigh, the man turned to Nakona.

"All right, then that'll be two-hundred-fifty majors," he said.

Nakona blinked. "That's a lot for a Ministry retirement stipend. How about we all chip in, yes?"

"I'll pay it!" I said, over the others' assent, but as they pressed around, pulling out wallets, the manager caught sight of Laloran-morna in the makeshift sling.

"Oh no," he said, backing away from the counter. "No no no. You're not taking him out on one of our boats. He looks like he's ready for intensive care, or—" He was polite enough to refrain from finishing the sentence.

"I'm his medical attendant," Ms. Bama began, but at that moment seawater bloomed on Laloran-morna's body, bloomed and effervesced, leaving behind white salt on dark skin. There was no puddle, no soaking clothing the way there usually was, and as if lifted by that brief sea swell, Laloran-morna was now standing.

"You don't need to fret, Sonny. I'm not going to die on your boat," he said.

The manager quailed.

"I'm from the Ministry of Divinities," I said. "We're on Ministry business."

"Is he— Is he—?" the manager stuttered.

"Yes," I said, though I wasn't at all sure who or what the manager thought Laloran-morna was. He clearly didn't have deep enough roots in the area to know the story of the old man who used to be a god and who sometimes sweated out whole puddles of ocean. But then, what had just happened didn't match that story, either. I shivered. "Here's my fund transfer code," I said, writing it on a scrap of paper, since I didn't have my unicom. "May we take the boat?"

"Yes, yes—please. Any of the three moored out there. They're all charged up. Oh! But here." He slid a map across the counter. "These areas here are fine, and here, but over here's off limits—that's where they're building that resort. And keep in sight of land at all time."

The other retired gods had settled themselves on the benches on either side of the boxy little boat. Only Laloran-morna was still walking, unassisted. Ms. Bama followed close by him, carrying the portable oxygen concentrator and saying things like "take it slowly" and "careful now," but he just laughed a voiceless laugh.

"It's all right, little daughter. I feel better than I have in a long time." Like it had at the boat rental, his skin glistened with seawater that disappeared almost before it could be perceived.

"I wouldn't mind a bit of sea-touch like that," remarked Anin, and Nakota and the others laughed.

"It's just like the other night," murmured Ms. Bama.

Laloran-morna sat down between Anin and Kadiuk, leaned back against the side of the boat, and closed his eyes. "They're for *her*. My waves."

I was focused on steering the boat, maneuvering it along the coast in the direction of the mangrove spit, on the edge of Daybreak Ventures' operations, but Ms. Bama's remark and Laloran-morna's reply snagged my attention.

"What do you mean, 'they're for her'?" I asked, an edge to my voice. "What waves?"

"*My* waves. I told you: I send my waves to her, with the lagoonfire."

I stopped the boat.

"Have you done this—have sent your waves to her—before now? Recently, I mean. Have you sent your waves to her since lagoonfire season began?" I looked from Laloran-morna to Ms. Bama. She nodded.

"Just one other time," she said. "Two nights ago. I was cutting the holy one some pineapple, and when I took it to him, I saw water appearing and vanishing, appearing and vanishing, leaving him white with salt, and salt in his pajamas and on his sleeping mat."

Two nights ago, when Daybreak Ventures' construction site had flooded.

So it had been Laloran-morna after all.

I came over to him and took his hands. What was it that Captain Lotuk suspected me of? Mangling his decommissioning for just such a purpose?

"Grandfather," I said.

Seawater oozed between my fingers and vanished, leaving them gritty with salt.

"Grandfather, you have to wait. Don't send your waves to Goblet just yet. She's not where you expect her."

"She can only be one place. She is the place. She's the Goblet," he replied.

"Please," I begged. "Just wait. Wait until you see her garden."

"Oh Sweeting, that garden... I haven't seen it in so long. I have to close my eyes to see it."

"You'll see it with your eyes open," I promised— recklessly. What did I have to work with? Ateni's hidden knot stones, a bag of jade mussels, and some dried slenderweed. With nothing more than those three items and the memories of the retired gods, I would have to conjure a garden I'd never seen.

"The manager was right. This is a terrible night for moon viewing," Nakona remarked. The last glimmers of twilight were dying away, and no hint of any stars could be seen through the thick layers of cloud. It was still hours before the moon would rise.

"But a good night for the lights of the city," observed Malirin, and it was true: the coast was spangled with lights that came together in a great ethereal web if you directed your eyes toward the center of the capital.

I went back to the little boat's helm. It wasn't lights but darkness I was looking for, a patch of darker darkness, ink strokes against the bruise-colored sky. And there it was, a thin line of silhouetted trees, their magnificent prop roots arching into the water. As we drew near, I heard a rough sound from underneath the boat. The lanterns strung along the boat's roof revealed the cause: seagrass, thick and undulating, that the boat was passing over.

"Now?" gasped Laloran-morna suddenly, as if wakened from a dream. "Is it time for me to send my waves?" The brief echo of divinity that had seemed to surround him back at the boat rental was gone—he was as weak or weaker than before.

"Not yet—soon."

"Can you put these pesky things out?" Kadiuk asked, waving a hand at the lanterns.

"There's still no moon to see—no stars, either," Nakona said.

Kadiuk snorted. "It's not the sky I'm interested in."

A dial allowed me to dim the lanterns; pressing the button in the center turned them off completely.

"Well now I can't see my hand even if I wave it in front of my face," Nakona complained.

Kadiuk twisted around and threw something that hit the water with plop. Faint, pale-blue light flashed on the water's surface.

"Lagoonfire!" said Anin.

"Lagoonfire," said Kadiuk, satisfaction in his voice. "All right, Sweeting, you can put the lights back on. I wouldn't want Nakona to poke herself in the eye."

Laloran-morna said nothing. His eyes were closed and his breathing labored.

"Lolo?" Anin touched his arm.

"It needs to be soon," Laloran-morna said at last, taking a breath between each word. "Sweeting? Soon? And you'll free Goblet? I should never...have kept her here."

His words were a vice closing on my heart. "Very soon," I said.

I steered the boat to a break in the mangroves. The wind was picking up — another downpour must have been nearing — and the boat rocked.

"Where are we?" Ms. Bama asked in a small voice.

"This isn't Cup of the Sea," said Kadiuk.

"But it will be," I said. "Everyone, stay on board. And try to remember everything you can about Lotus Estuary — Cup of the Sea."

I jumped from the boat as far onto shore as I could and managed to hit firm ground. First things first: I wanted to find the knot stones Ateni had hidden here. He had said they were heavy, and he would have been coming from the other side of the spit — the Daybreak Ventures side. But he also wouldn't have wanted them to be easily visible... I hopped from prop root to prop root in the dim no-light of the overcast night, growing gradually more desperate. How big a thing was I looking for? What if I couldn't find them? Could I conjure ancient Cup of the Sea without them?

Next leap I stumbled, fell into the mud. Where I broke the water it glowed, and in that glow, I saw a smooth, rounded shape with a hole carved into it near the top, a space through which ropes could pass... This was one of one of Ateni's knot stones. How had he ever wrestled this thing into a moto-canoe? It was half-sunk in the mud and still reached to my knee. I ran my hand over the top, by the hole. Yes, these indentations, surely if seen in daylight they would form a Laloran-morna knot. No, a Goblet knot. Did she know? Did she mind that her devotees' custom had been taken over by newcomers? Did Laloran-morna feel sorry for that? Had he ever thought that the increase in his own worshipers might have been at the expense of his beloved? He blamed himself for tethering her to this world, but was he in part responsible for her fading in the first place?

I couldn't think about that now. I fumbled in my bag, pushed aside the jade mussels and the packet of slenderweed until my fingers found a bead of divine resin. My hand closed in a fist around it. I spoke the names of the Sweet Harbor gods—not just Malirin, Laloran-morna, Anin, Nakona, and Kadiuk, but the ones who had already passed away, and then, as the bead grew warm in my hand, the names of the Abstractions most relevant for this decommissioning: Memory, Justice, Devotion, Love, Duty, History, Divinity. Just as the bead began to smoke, I placed it on the knot stone. Then I shook a couple of jade mussels out onto the stone, ripped open the package of dried slenderweed, pulled out a few brittle strands, and placed them underneath the jade mussels so they wouldn't blow away.

Now to find the other two knot stones. Surely Ateni wouldn't have wasted time and effort trying to hide them at a distance, I thought to myself, but it was so dark!

"Goddess—Goblet. I could use your help," I whispered.

Nothing.

Fortunately, I stumbled across the other two after not too much longer, repeated the process, and tripped and stumbled my way back to the boat.

"Ms. Sweeting—is that you?" called Ms. Bama.

"Yes—it's time to disembark."

Remarkably, Nakona and Kadiuk had no problem jumping over the soft mud, just as I had. Ms. Bama I had had no doubts would manage it. But Malirin and Anin were carrying Laloran-morna and had to step right into its grasp. Down they sank—but Kaduik and I grabbed Malirin's free arm, and Ms. Bama and Nakona grabbed Anin's, and soon all of us were standing on more or less firm ground.

No one spoke, but it wasn't quiet. A shimmer of insect song hung in the air, and tree frogs chirping and whistling to one another like birds. And quite near, the familiar whine of mosquitoes.

I had two more divine resin beads in my hands, and as I murmured the Sweet Harbor gods' names, they grew hot, and when smoke was rising from them, I put them on the ground several paces away from us, then repeated the process until we were standing in a bounded, sanctified space. I placed the remaining jade mussels and slenderweed on the edge of the space closest to the direction in which the knot stones lay.

"This is the Cup of the Sea," I intoned. "Jade mussels and slenderweed are burgeoning on the ropes secured to the great stones. Crabs flourish among the mangroves, and clams sleep in the silt."

The heavy scent of the divine resin hung in the humid air.

"The tide is coming in; it's nearly high," I continued. "Grandfather, call your warm waves now. Fill the cup with lagoonfire, so all the little creatures can feast."

Laloran-morna, who had been clinging so tenuously to consciousness, stood up. Seawater shimmered on his skin and vanished, shimmered and vanished, glowing eerie blue — lagoonfire. Waves broke on the shore, broke closer. Water streamed in under our feet, then over our feet.

In the distance there was a hum and a rhythmic chug, familiar somehow.

"Kadiuk-grandfather," I said, "Tell us what we see."

The hum and chug grew louder.

"Not many gardeners are working now," Kadiuk said, voice dreamy. "They'll wait for low tide. Just children splashing in the shallows and budding young men, practicing swimming into the current. At night they'll dive under, seek lagoonfire blessing on their manhood. Slenderweed is drying on lines strung in the trees. There's a pile of seagrass hay, and three men are tying it into bundles, getting ready to build a new house. A woman's singing..."

It was coming into being, ancient thousand-year-old daylight, waters glinting in the sun, whoops and laughter from the children. The gusts of wind, the sudden shower of rain in our own reality didn't disturb the vision, even as our clothes soaked through, even as the waves Laloran-morna summoned brought water to our knees.

Then in our own reality, the hum and chug I'd been dimly aware of abruptly stopped.

"Thirty-Seven, in the name of all that's holy, what do you think you're doing? Are you attempting a redeification of Laloran-morna?"

Another Fairest Moonlight electraboat had pulled in alongside ours. On it were Five and Tailin. Everyone turned when Five spoke, and the vision of Cup of the Sea melted away. The two disembarked, stepping directly into the gulping mud. Nakona and Ms. Bama pulled first one, then the other free. Five strode up to within a hair's breadth of my face — we stood nose to nose.

"What is this insanity?" she demanded.

"I'm going to decommission Laloran-morna's lover, the way I promised I would," I said doggedly.

"This doesn't look like a decommissioning," Five retorted, arm extended, offering in evidence Laloran-morna, standing unaided but trancelike, an otherworldly glow around him that pulsed with each bloom and lifting of seawater from his skin. "Tailin told me Laloran-morna was on death's door — this man is not on death's door. This *man* doesn't seem mortal at all."

"This—this is how he is," I stuttered. "You remember the problems with his decommissioning—how I didn't quite—how there were aftereffects."

"Yes, the seawater when his emotions run high. But this isn't that—is it. He's summoning waves. Mortals don't summon waves."

The light around Laloran-morna was dimming, the trance lifting. I thought of how weak he'd been on the boat. He might not survive another descent from whatever this state was.

"Yes, but you have to believe me: I'm not recommissioning him, and his calling the waves—it's necessary for decommissioning this other goddess. The waves are how she finds him—maybe how she finds herself. She was a tutelary goddess of Cup of...of Lotus Estuary, but the estuary's gone now, so we're creating it here. If you try to stop us, then Laloran-morna's just going to die, and the goddess is going to be left behind. We'll have no way of reaching her or decommissioning her.

"The goddess you thought might be making trouble for Daybreak Ventures," said Five slowly.

"That's right." I wasn't about to let on that Laloran-morna was likely the culprit after all—not if Five herself hadn't reached that conclusion, seeing waves rise and vanish from his body.

"Ms. Sweeting!" Ms. Bama's voice shook. "The holy one..." She was struggling to support Laloran-morna, who was slumped against her.

"Go to him. Help him," Five ordered. "Thirty-Three and I will reestablish—what's the name again?"

"Lotus Estuary," I repeated. And to Tailin, "There's slenderweed and jade mussels at each of the bounding points. All the Sweet Harbor gods remember the place, but Kadiuk in particular." Tailin set about reinforcing the sacred space while Five enjoined the Sweet Harbor gods to envision the estuary.

I knelt in the water, and between us, Ms. Bama and I carefully lowered Laloran-morna into my receiving lap. I put a hand on his chest but couldn't feel a rise or fall.

"Don't leave now," I begged.

It was so dark. The lights from the electraboats had disappeared, lost in the vision of Cup of the Sea the retired gods were summoning, guided by Five and Tailin: this time the estuary at night, its waters glowing where they lapped the shore and whenever a fish broke the surface.

"Please open your eyes," I pleaded. "The Cup of the Sea—the Goblet—is brimming with lagoonfire. Don't you want to see her? Don't you have something to tell her?"

"I'm too tired, Sweeting. You'll have tell her. You know what I want to say." His lips weren't moving; he was speaking as gods often do, mind to mind, heart to heart.

Then we heard a new voice, speaking in the same manner.

"What games you play, Lagoonfire, sending me these fruitful waves, and then, when I awake and come to you, you're in the arms of a rival. And isn't it the very one who thrust you into mortality?"

Goblet rose from the water — she was the water, and the silt below the water — in the form of a woman, dark and beautiful, naked save for garlands of jade mussels about her neck and girdling her waist. Pale ripples of light swept over her skin and receded like breaking waves.

"I needed her," Laloran-morna replied. "I couldn't come to you by myself — I have no strength, no breath. My time in mortality is ending."

He still lay inert, his head resting in the crook of my neck, but a vision-figure of him in the prime of life rose up, dressed not in the cloak and wrap I remembered from childhood representations, but in a pandanus-leaf skirt — the ancient clothing of the islanders of the Coral Archipelagos. He went to Goblet, who smiled in welcome, and made to gather her hands in his, but the vision-figure had no substance and couldn't grasp them. Goblet's smile faded.

"And so you'll close your eyes and sleep, and never wake again?" she cried. "No, no. Come back into immortality, and let's go share stories and other things, the way we always have. You were foolish ever to leave."

"I can't, dearest love. My divinity was falling away even before Sweeting put the mortal verdict on me. There's nothing for me to go back to—no prayers, no offerings, no fear, no awe."

"This is why I tried to keep you," Goblet said, pain in her voice. "Why didn't I succeed? How did it come to pass that I should be weaker than a creature like her, as insubstantial as morning dew?"

"You tried to keep me? No, love: I tried to keep *you* — to my shame. But I was lonely. That's my excuse. I couldn't bear to see you go."

"Why do you say that, when I'm always here? Look!" She spread her arms, and light shimmered in the water of the vision-estuary, an inverse shadow. "Is it not so?"

"Not so," echoed Laloran-morna, the words heavy. "The waters, yes, the shore…but not the garden, not the people, not the you whom I could talk to, the way we're talking now. The you whom I could—"

The force of Laloran-morna's desire rushed through me, and for a moment I saw Goblet the way he did—her lips, her skin, each inward bend, each outward curve. Ms. Bama gasped. I think she felt it too. I suspect we all did.

Goblet's gaze grew distant.

"You're right," she said, after a moment. "The people have all gone to sleep. They, and their children, and their children's children, and on and on." She met Laloran-morna's eyes. "How is it that I haven't known this?" A pause. "Have I been asleep, Lagoonfire? We meet, we laugh, I breathe in your stories and you mine...and then what, lover? I have no memory."

"I prayed to you," Laloran-morna said. "I set out dried fingerlings for you and poured palm wine into your waters. I sang the songs your people used to sing of you, and doing that, I kept you from leaving me entirely. But you only ever come to me in lagoonfire season. You only awaken when I send these potent waves to you."

Goblet frowned, and a gust of wind moved over the face of the vision-estuary — and also set the leaves of the mangroves outside the sacred space rustling.

"How's that happening?" I heard Tailin ask. "She's not connected with the weather, and neither is Laloran-morna."

"One time only I awoke without those waves," Goblet recalled. "It was because I felt life rushing from me. That was you, lover. You were leaving me — following her. I tried to hold you, but I couldn't. So I bade my waters to stay with you and to lead you back to me. I couldn't leave you wholly mortal."

So it wasn't my faulty decommissioning that had caused Laloran-morna's irregularities. That had been Goblet's doing: she had endowed Laloran-morna with some portion of the godhead he had preserved in her — right as I was trying to separate him from it. I ought to have felt vindicated, but instead I felt bereft.

The god of warm waves and the estuary goddess stared at each other, twin expressions on their faces.

"I asked her to bring me here because I couldn't come on my own," Laloran-morna repeated, "but also because she can do for you as she did for me — save you from being trapped as a wraith with a forgotten name, after I'm gone."

Goblet turned her head sharply, a gesture of refusal, and the garlands of green-tipped shells about her neck clacked together.

"Accept frailty, illness, and pain — why would you offer this?"

Laloran-morna looked crestfallen. "Those parts are drawbacks, yes, but there's more to it than that. Much more." He looked to the other Sweet Harbor gods for support.

"The mortals have diverting games of strategy you can play to pass the time," Anin said.

"And they crush fruits to make extraordinary drinks," said Nakona. "Experiencing juice as a mortal is different from receiving a libation. Much more, mmm, sensual."

"The little ones are fun to watch. It's not like how we used to watch them—it's like watching from the inside," said Kadiuk.

Goblet's eyes widened when he spoke. "Kadiuk—little crab, I remember you."

"I remember you too, Cup of the Sea," Kadiuk replied, smiling, then dropping his gaze, shy as a child.

"And you make friends with them," put in Laloran-morna. "That's also different, once you're mortal yourself." His spirit-form gazed back at me and Ms. Bama. This was possibly a mistake, as Goblet crossed her arms and raised an eyebrow.

"I am the Cup of the Sea." she declared. "If *this* must fade"—she indicated the form she had adopted—"still I survive." Then, coaxingly, "come join me. Be the waters with me, the silt, the rocks."

"Ah, dear love," Laloran-morna said, each word sorrow laden, "no. It's gone. Cup of the Sea is gone." He turned to me for confirmation.

I swallowed, nodded. "He's right. There is no estuary now. The river's been diverted and the delta land drained and filled."

Another gust of wind pelted my face with rain, and I flinched, but Goblet was laughing.

"What a story!" she said. "If it's so, little dewdrop, then what do I see before me here?"

"We conjured it for you," I replied. "So you could find Grandfather. So you'd come."

Goblet's expression was distant again for a moment, and then a look of shock overspread her face. My throat constricted at the sight.

And then the wind was suddenly roaring around us, and a wave nearly knocked me down, would have pulled Laloran-morna's body from my arms if Ms. Bama and Anin hadn't come to my aid. The vision of Cup of the Sea shredded and vanished.

"That was a deceitful trick," Goblet said coldly. She turned to Laloran-morna's spirit form. "Lagoonfire, you must undo the damage that's been done to me. I'll lend you my strength, but send your waves. Restore me."

"Thirty-Seven, Thirty-Three, this has just become an adversarial decommissioning, and we'll have to finish it now, before this goddess can do any more damage!" That was Five, voice firm and clear over the wind and rain. "Speak with me now, 'We, gathered—'"

"No, wait!" I said. "Goblet, please: the place you want to send your waves—there are people there, workers, who—"

"Destroyed me," Goblet said.

"They didn't know," I said miserably. "Nobody knew. You yourself didn't know—you'd be asleep if it weren't for—"

Goblet turned to Laloran-morna. "Restore me," she demanded.

"Dearest love, those workers are my children's children's children. I don't want to harm them."

Tailin was joining Five, speaking the words for an adversarial decommissioning.

"Goblet, they're your children too!" I cried out. Tailin broke off, and in the electraboats' lurching light I caught his look of surprise.

"All my children have fallen asleep," Goblet answered, but she hesitated. Her eyes grew distant once again. Then suddenly the wind fell away and the rain lifted.

"It's true," Goblet murmured. "They *are* my children. Not all, but many. And you, too," she said, looking me over in wonder. She turned to Ms. Bama. "And you."

Five had gone silent. It was to her that Goblet turned next. "Even you," Goblet said. "Such a faint tie, but I feel it." Her eyes fell last on Tailin. "But not you."

"My family's from far inland," he muttered. "I'm the first to come to the capital."

"What do I do now?" Goblet asked me, all imperiousness gone. "I don't think I can become a mortal human."

"Not all decommissioned gods take human form," said Five. "Other tutelary deities sink back into the place they arose from."

"But how can I do that, when I've been unmade?"

I was alarmed to see tears overflow her eyes and spill down her cheeks. The glow of lagoonfire rippling over her skin lingered in their tracks. And then I knew the answer.

"Sink into the lagoonfire," I said.

"Thirty-Seven!" said Five sharply, at once a warning and a reprimand, but Goblet smiled a dazzling smile.

"Yes. I'll become the gift you gave me, lover," she said, turning back to where the vision-figure of Laloran-morna had stood—but he was gone. The old man in my arms gave a sudden start and gulped air.

His eyes met Goblet's, and he smiled. "That's perfect, dearest love."

And before I or Five or Tailin could say a word, let alone intone her decommissioning, Goblet had vanished, and Laloran-morna had released a long last breath. I hugged him tight.

"Brother!" cried Anin, all desolation. Beside me, Ms. Bama wept.

A blinding searchlight cut through our grief. It came from a sleek vessel whose approach had gone unnoticed by all of us. Silhouetted on its deck were a dozen figures, one with a megaphone. Another light, coming from the opposite side of the spit, caught us from behind, creating long shadows that reached out for the eletraboats and then vanished as the light passed by.

"I'd like you all to assemble on the boat to your left," said the figure with the megaphone. It was Captain Lotuk. Five and Tailin exchanged appalled looks. Ms. Bama stilled, wet eyelashes and puffy eyes sharply defined in the merciless light.

"So disrespectful," muttered Nakona.

"They're armed," observed Malirin.

In short order we were all aboard one of the electraboats. A gangplank was extended from the Civil Order vessel, and Captain Lotuk and several of her subordinates came over. Two examined Laloran-morna, pronounced him dead, and took his body back to their vessel. Even Nakona was too cowed to object or ask any questions. We all took seats on one side of the boat, and although the night was not that cool, all of us were soaked to the skin, and we leaned in close to one another share a little warmth. Even so, I clenched my teeth to keep them from chattering.

Nobody spoke. Captain Lotuk's gaze rested contemplatively on us all for several heartbeats.

"Let's start with you, shall we, Ms. Kiukai? I believe you're the highest-ranking person here."

It was a shock to hear Five addressed by her name. The top officials in any of the Ministry's departments generally get called by their rank wherever they go. She was Decommissioner Five.

"I believe you told me, when last we spoke, that Ms. Manu's persistent interest in the Daybreak Ventures incident was not officially sanctioned, and that you had, in fact, issued a reprimand. And yet here you are, at night, on Daybreak Ventures' property, with Ms. Manu. Can you explain that to me?"

Five cleared her throat. "I received a communication from Decommissioner Thirty-Three—Mr. Kele here. He was worried about her. She's been preoccupied with the health of Laloran-morna, the retired god whom Civil Order requested the Ministry to check up on in connection with the Daybreak Ventures incident. We knew Thirty-Seven—Ms. Manu—wanted to see him a last time before he passed away. Earlier she'd said some things to me about accommodating the retired god's last wishes that alarmed me, and from what Thirty-Three told me, I was afraid she might be trying to act on those wishes." Five took a breath. "I wanted to stop her before she could get herself in any trouble."

"Imagine respect for an elder's last wishes being a possible offense," Nakona said to Kaduik in an exaggerated whisper. Captain Lotuk ignored her.

"And you didn't think to get in touch with me? After everything I told you about Ms. Manu's personal history and possible risks?"

"Whatever her background, she's always been... She's never... I know Thirty-Seven. I just didn't think it was possible that she—"

"You just didn't think," repeated Captain Lotuk gravely. "Let me ask you something: do you think I, as a captain in Civil Order, ought to be making decisions regarding worship of the Polity's gods and goddesses?"

Five's lips thinned, a sure sign of her irritation at being taken down this rhetorical path.

"No," she said.

Captain Lotuk's brief smile was her only acknowledgment of triumph.

"Right. And by that same reasoning, you, a Ministry of Divinities bureaucrat, need to leave decisions on the Polity's internal security to me and my colleagues. I did ask you to call if anything seemed untoward."

Five gave a formal nod. "Yes, Captain. It was a mistake not to."

Captain Lotuk turned to Tailin. "And you, Mr. Kele. You were worried about Ms. Manu? Why, precisely?"

"Three of us had agreed to go out together in the evening, and then she said that she couldn't stay, that she needed to see Laloran-morna, and-and... I just was worried," Tailin said evasively, eyes on his hands, which were clasped tightly in his lap.

"But that's not why you contacted your superior, is it. Ms. Manu left you something," Captain Lotuk prompted.

Tailin looked up, startled.

"'Incomplete honesty is dishonesty.'" It was another Thought Orthodoxy maxim. "Did you know what she had left you?"

"It was something for her apartment manager," Tailin said, barely audible. "Paperwork, she said. But when I took off my jacket, I noticed a light blinking through the envelope, same pattern as a unicom new-messages alert, if you've muted the chime." He looked very unhappy. "I didn't want to pry into Thirty-Seven's business, but if she'd gone and done something crazy... So I opened it, and" —he shrugged helplessly—"it was her unicom." He held the envelope out to me.

"Here," he said. "You have six messages." He looked away quickly.

I slipped my unicom back on my wrist and tapped it to call up the messages. Five anxious ones from Ms. Bama and one querulous one from Nakona.

"You're probably aware from crime dramas that when necessary, Civil Order can track a unicom," Captain Lotuk was saying. "Ms. Manu certainly was. That's why she left hers with you, to evade tracking. She didn't realize that if Civil Order activates tracking, all the other unicoms in the area also register." Her minute smile returned. "Two unicom signals virtually on top of each other in a public area is a red flag. Maybe it's just a couple holding hands. Or maybe it's something like this."

Captain Lotuk turned to me. "Which brings us to you, Ms. Manu."

At her words, I felt as if someone had placed a lead blanket over my shoulders, and with that weight came a deep hopelessness. I could shape thoughts about Laloran-morna, could tell myself that at least I had seen him reunited with Goblet before he died, but there was no joy or pride there, just a dull ache that must be grief, or would become grief. And then there was everything else. I had put Five and Tailin in Civil Order's sights. I had destroyed my grandparents' careful efforts to secure my future. And yet possibly I'd also been wronging my parents all my life. And what about Ateni? With Captain Lotuk standing over me, it suddenly was clear to me that my actions weren't going to set him free, would never have been able to do that. Even if Tailin and Five attested to Goblet's desire to send waves to Lotus Estuary tonight, Captain Lotuk could still stand by her story of a bomb two days ago. Proof and evidence were only relevant if she accepted them.

"Ms. Manu!"

It was the third time she'd said my name.

"I'm sorry," I murmured. "Sometimes interacting with deities can cause grogginess."

"It's been a long night. I'll keep this brief. When it came to my attention that you met Mr. Ninin on Daybreak Ventures' property while supposedly on your Ministry assignment, it raised my suspicions. Your background, his background — it seemed possible the flooding was part of a plot, a trial run for something bigger, something involving weaponizing a former god. We apprehended Mr. Ninin but left you free to see if you'd lead us to other coconspirators."

I felt as if a piece of glowing charcoal had become lodged in my stomach.

"When Mr. Ninin's delinquent foster brother went running after you this afternoon, it seemed my suspicions were confirmed," she continued. "But when I had him brought in, the most remarkable thing happened: even with the offer of an expedited vendor's license and cart rental in exchange for information about your plans, all I could get from him was that you were a brainwashed tool of the Polity!" Her lips quirked, but then her face grew thoughtful. "He said you vigorously rejected the 'truths' he tried to share with you. Very interesting, very impressive that someone with your background should be so stalwart. It made me rather more curious about your claims about the flooding.

"We continued with long-distance monitoring, and then shortly after you set out from Fairest Moonlight's docks, I was given word of a new seawater incursion at Daybreak Ventures' construction site, only to be told in the next minute that it had stopped, that—this was what the reporting officers said— 'it was like someone shook the sea smooth.' And instead the waters rose here. Quite remarkable. You appear to have redirected the waves here, or I suppose I should say you induced the retired god to redirect them—or got your superior to do so," she amended, some after-the-fact deference to Five.

This shift in tenor confused me.

Captain Lotuk smiled. "You saved the construction site. Well done."

I should have registered something, relief at the very least, but there was nothing. I can't even recall if I thanked her. The others were equally silent, but Captain Lotuk took it in stride.

"You'll find a summons on your unicom," she told me. "There's some follow-up to attend to. And I'll be in touch with you two as well," she said to Tailin and Five. "For now, I think we're done here. Oh, and I'm very sorry for your loss. I'll be sure the retired god's body is returned to...?"

"Sweet Harbor Compassionate Care Associates," said Ms. Bama huskily.

Captain Lotuk nodded, and then she and her officers departed on the Civil Order vessel, and we were left, mute and heavy as Ateni's knot stones. Eventually Five murmured to Tailin that they had better get back on their own boat. We all still needed to return to Fairest Moonlight Electraboat Rentals. With the rest of us as a counterweight, she leaned over the rail of our boat, grabbed the rail of theirs, and swung herself over, then went to the helm. The boat's engine sprang to life.

Before following, Tailin turned to me, troubled.

"What you said to Goblet, about the Daybreak Ventures workers being her children too...didn't you tell me you thought she was a deity of...?" He kept his voice was low, so as not to be overheard, and he didn't finish his sentence, but I knew what he was asking.

"She is," I said. "I'm sure of it."

He closed his eyes.

"Thirty-Three, we need to go," Five called.

"You know as far as Five's concerned, she's just a forgotten Sweet Harbor goddess—a Sea Traveler goddess," Tailin said, speaking quickly now, still for my ears only.

"Only because Five hasn't—"

"Thirty-Seven! Sae. Please don't push it. We're already facing enough fallout as it is. And you promised." Such controlled desperation in those words.

Proud Goblet, lovestruck Laloran-morna. The tidal garden, the estuary—all gone. But not entirely. Nothing was finished, not yet.

"I won't say anything," I said. *But one day, things will be different.*

"Now is not the time or place for a private conference," said Five, coming near. "Do you need a hand, Thirty-Three?"

Tailin gave me a brief nod, then took Five's offered hand and crossed to the other boat.

It wasn't the parting I wanted, but there was no help for it.

A notice of the passing of Laloran-morna, former god of warm waves, went out through news channels in all formats, and the Garden of Remembrance in Sweet Harbor District was thronged with those who remembered the stories their parents or grandparents had shared. It moved me to see that sea of faces. Later, those of us who had shared his final hours took a boat out to open waters to cast his ashes there. *Sink into lagoonfire, Lagoonfire,* I prayed, in my heart joining him with Goblet.

Goblet, whom Five fretted over. Had the decommissioning been successful? The goddess had disappeared so precipitously. Five sought and received permission from Daybreak Ventures to conduct a sealing ceremony at the mangrove spit, an extra formality she insisted on just to be sure. I wasn't part of the team that performed it.

But even before those events, I had a summons to Civil Order's West Ward offices to attend to. I thought going there might be easier this time around, since I had some idea of what to expect, but it wasn't. It's not just your own fears you have to deal with in a place like that, it's the accumulated disquiet of all the people who've gone before you. The walls, benches, and floor of the reception hall are drenched in anxiety—they exude it like an unpleasant odor. But I walked up the aisle, showed my summons to the officer on duty, waited to be called, and then, just like last time, Captain Lotuk appeared and led me to her little office.

Like last time, she poured me a class of lemon water. She sat, fingers interlaced before her on her desk, watching me silently as I took a few sips.

"It's good to see you again," she said when I set down the glass, and I relaxed a fraction.

"I was so close to arresting you after you ditched your unicorn," she remarked conversationally, and my fears came racing back.

"But then you pulled off that impressive save at the Daybreak Ventures site," she continued.

I took another sip of water, feeling seasick.

"All the decommissioning-related business — that's all taken care of, I gather? What'll it be like for your department when the Ministry of Divinities moves entirely to Abstractions? Do Abstractions even get decommissioned?"

"No — they can be deprioritized, or what constitutes an Abstraction can be redefined," I replied, wondering where the small talk was leading.

"Mmm." She was back to staring at me. I tried not to fidget.

"We're releasing Mr. Ninin," she said, and smiled at my sharp intake of breath.

"I thought you'd be pleased. There are some riders and stipulations—some rehabilitation and reeducation classes he'll need to attend, but it won't require confinement."

Anger lanced through me. *Won't require confinement? They should never have detained him in the first place.* Captain Lotuk raised an eyebrow, and I schooled my expression.

"That's better," she said quietly. After a brief pause, she said, "Standard protocols dictate that the two of you should have nothing to do with each other henceforth. You're too likely to make trouble for each other. But!" she continued, raising a hand when I started to protest, "there's a way around that. You can see Mr. Ninin all you like, if you're willing to give me reports on his activities and the activities of his associates."

I was dumbfounded. "I can see him if I spy for you? You want me to be a rat?"

"My family's ancestral village was protected by a rat spirit. Rats are clever, loving, and loyal animals whom we could all benefit from emulating," Captain Lotuk returned, "but no, what I'm suggesting isn't spying. It's more along the lines of a diary, a progress report."

"Like my grandparents had to keep, when I was little?" I asked bitterly. "They did, didn't they—have to report on me."

"Anyone who adopted or fostered a Fifteen Breezes orphan had to," Captan Lotuk replied. "Your case wasn't unique."

I snorted. "It was, though."

We stared at each other, me furious, and her with something like pity on her face.

"That foster brother of Mr. Ninin's really got under your skin," she said.

"Were the other things he said true?" I hadn't meant to speak that question aloud, but with Captain Lotuk's shocked eyes on me, I plunged ahead, heart racing. "The things about my parents? About what happened that night at Fifteen Breezes?"

The captain stood up abruptly, planted her palms on the desk, and leaned across it. I shrank back.

"Have you forgotten who you're talking to? Where you *are?* I don't doubt you'd like to escape the burden of your parents' crimes, but if you think I'm going to validate that delinquent's nonsense, you're sorely mistaken. I'm not going to indulge you."

"A-and I'm not going to be a spy!" I shot back, silently cursing the tears that were now streaming down my cheeks.

Captain Lotuk sighed, sat back down, and pushed a box of tissues toward me.

"As you wish. But you realize that means you're forfeiting the possibility of staying in touch with Mr. Ninin."

"Fine," I said, wiping my eyes and blowing my nose. *There will be ways around this prohibition,* I thought grimly. *I just need to find them.*

"And it will be very bad for both of you if you're found to be fraternizing," she said.

I crossed my arms and scowled.

"There's also the matter of sanctions for your colleagues, Ms. Kiukai and Mr. Kele," she said, opening a folder.

"What do you mean, sanctions? What sanctions? I thought they were only getting reprimands."

"The reprimands are for their misjudgments relating to the current case, but with the way you're behaving now, it seems sanctions are in order for failure to recognize and correct your recalcitrant tendencies."

"I see. You're going to hurt them to punish me." I thought of hardworking Five and dedicated Tailin and seethed with helpless anger.

Captain Lotuk gave a short laugh. "I assure you, this is not what punishment looks like. And before you say it: it's not a threat or an attempt at coercion, either. It's simply a natural consequence of your behavior. If you're helpful and make the common good your priority, it speaks favorably of your colleagues' influence and demonstrates that you'd be a beneficial influence on Mr. Ninin. If you're uncooperative, childish, and traffic in stories that damage the common good, it speaks poorly of your colleagues and makes you someone who absolutely should not be allowed near —"

"Oh please just stop!" I cried, my hands involuntarily flying to my ears. Hastily I put them in my lap, two tight fists, and said, "I apologize — I'm sorry. I understand. I was wrong. I'll do — what you said."

"But you just said you wouldn't. You seemed quite sure. So the offer is rescinded." Her gaze was steady, cool.

I imagined jumping to my feet just like she'd done, imagined leaning across the desk and putting my hands around her neck and squeezing, squeezing so hard... Pain in the palms of my hands brought me back to myself — my nails digging into them. I took a breath, kept my voice calm.

"I just don't want Five and Tailin to suffer because of what I've done — or am doing — or —"

"But people do suffer because of the actions of others. You know that."

"Yes, all right, you're right, I do know that, but I don't want to add to it! I want to make up for it. Please?" I hated myself and Captain Lotuk in equal measure at that moment. The captain, unperturbed, appeared to be considering my words.

"All right," she said. "Let's give it a try. You could be the perfect person for this if you attend to it diligently, but I'm also going to sign you up for a six-week reaffirmation course, just so you can brush up on Thought Orthodoxy, civic virtue, and so on."

"I really don't think I need that—I think I probably still have the entire Thought Orthodoxy curriculum memorized, and—"

"A refresher never hurts," interrupted Captain Lotuk. "Everyone in Civil Order has to take one every six months or so. It'll be good for you. It'll help you see things more clearly. If it makes you feel any better, I was going to sign you up for one regardless of how things went with the other business. All right?"

I gritted my teeth and nodded. "And Five and Tailin?" I asked.

Captain Lotuk smiled. "Clearly you're someone who acknowledges mistakes and seeks to improve. That speaks well of Ms. Kiukai and Mr. Kele, so their cases will close with just the reprimands."

I nodded, and Captain Lotuk escorted me out. I had the distinct impression that not only had she expected every turn our conversation had taken, but that she had orchestrated them.

Two months later, on a restday, I was sitting with the retired Sweet Harbor gods in the park by Promise of Unity Primary School when Ateni walked up. It was our first time to see each other since that day at the Civil Order offices. I introduced him and explained who he was, and the gods made much of him, especially Kadiuk. "We should talk, son. I have stories to share with you," he said, an offer Ateni fervently accepted. Then Ateni and I excused ourselves and walked awhile together.

"I've been trying to find you," Ateni said. "I didn't want to make trouble for you at your work—and I'm feeling shy of government buildings these days—so I didn't ask at the Ministry of Divinities. I figured the retired Sweet Harbor gods would know where to find you, and one of my former students said he does a lot of business selling juice to them in this park." He looked back over his shoulder at Mr. Tamlo, who waved at us. "And here you are." He ran a hand through his mop of hair—a gesture I remembered from before. "When I got released, they told me you had my contact information, but I haven't heard from you."

It wasn't an accusation, and Ateni didn't even sound particularly aggrieved, just tentative. Like he didn't want to push for the friendship we might have started if circumstances had been different.

"I've been putting it off," I said, avoiding his eyes. I watched my feet instead. *Look at them, clever things.* They avoided the big puddle, stepped over the toy earthmover that the park custodial team must have left there, against regulations, so the child it belonged to would have a chance to find and retrieve it. "Civil Order told me if I was going to have any contact with you, I had to report on you." I confessed. Then, because incomplete honesty is dishonesty, I added, "And I agreed." I stole a glance at him, but he appeared to be as interested in his feet as I'd been in mine.

"They were going to take it out on my colleagues if I said no," I continued. He still didn't speak or look up.

"So I was thinking—I was hoping—we could meet a few times, chat about your classes, the weather, whatever, and then just get together less and less frequently, and I could say, you know, that we just drifted apart," I concluded, feeling miserable. "I'm sorry."

"You were in an impossible situation," he said, so quietly he seemed almost to be talking to himself.

I shook my head. "I could have made a different choice. I'm just—I'm as bad as your foster brother thinks I am."

Ateni exhaled a laugh. "Paru just wants a hero, and the world keeps failing to deliver. Don't fault yourself for not meeting his standard." He stopped walking and looked me in the eye. "He's right about some things, though. Do you understand what I'm saying? He's right about some things."

"Captain Lotuk called his stories nonsense," I murmured, tears springing to my eyes.

"She would. But insulting the sun doesn't make it less bright. People from the old neighborhoods—they all know the truth. No one talks about it, but they know." He grabbed my hand and squeezed it, and I saw there were tears in his eyes, too. Before we knew it, we were holding each other tight, both of us children again, clinging to each other in the face of something overwhelming, too terrible to understand. And then equally suddenly, we pulled apart, wiped our faces, looked away.

"I'm glad you made the decision you did," Ateni said presently.

"I wasn't even sure you'd want to see me again," I said. "If we hadn't run into each other that day, they never would have detained you."

"Sure they would have," he said. "Our meeting may have given them an extra scare, but they were going to detain me anyway. I know that now. I didn't realize it back then—I was so naïve. I had no idea they'd care so much about a heterodox historical excavation theory." He hunched his shoulders. "It's not so much that I believed it but that I taught it. They really didn't like my spreading the Mudhugger thesis around. Said I was perpetrating a kind of fraud."

I digested this, thinking about what Tailin had said about the Committee on Thought Orthodoxy's likely reaction to a hypothetical Mudhugger civilization.

"In the record of Goblet's decommissioning, the Ministry's going to list her as a hitherto unacknowledged Sweet Harbor goddess," I said. "Nothing about her origins or who worshiped her." I sighed. "I wish you could have seen the memory-vision we conjured of Lotus Estuary. Your knot stones were part of a tidal garden. It was beautiful... Will you keep researching?"

"Oh yes," he said promptly. Then, with a half-smile, "Are you going to be reporting that to the captain?

That hurt. "I'm sure there's an innocuous way I can phrase it," I said, and we both managed a laugh.

"What about your students?" I asked. "They were so worried about you—they must be relieved you're free." Then I recalled the rehabilitation and reeducation classes Captain Lotuk had mentioned. "Or are you still...busy?"

Ateni smiled tightly. "I'm all rehabilitated now. 'Education is a precious gift, and it's wrong use it to spread deception or as a means of self-aggrandizement,'" he recited. He turned to me suddenly, chagrin on his face. "It was self-aggrandizement, a little bit. The press conference, anyway. I wanted the whole Polity to know what I'd discovered. Me, Ninin Ateni... The instructors at the rehabilitation and reeducation center said it was a real breakthrough when I admitted that."

He pulled a red leaf from a poinsettia bush, which sprinkled us with raindrops on its recoil, and started shredding the leaf along its veins. "They suggested that it would be better if I didn't teach ancient history or historical excavation anymore."

"What?" The wrongness of it took my breath away.

At Ateni's feet, the thin, red pieces of torn poinsettia leaf looked like bird feathers.

"It's all right. The Institute's going to keep me on as a literacy tutor. I'll be helping people who really have a need. But even that has a catch—can you guess?" Ateni looked unhappy.

"No. What is it?"

"I have to file reports on any contact I have with *you*."

Of course. Captain Lotuk's face, wearing its small smile, flashed in my mind.

"Well. I guess that's only fair," I said. Our eyes met, and we both started laughing, the kind of laughter that comes when you're too shattered to weep.

"We'll get through this somehow," I said, after we'd recovered.

"Let's see each other often and do a whole lot of nothing—we'll overwhelm the captain with paperwork, bore her with inconsequential details," he said.

I giggled. Then an idea seized me. "If you do keep researching, and if we report on it just right, maybe we can win her over to the Mudhugger thesis without her even realizing what's happening. Undetectable reeducation."

Ateni laughed uncomfortably and looked away. "I don't know," he said. "That seems...difficult." I felt a pang. He'd already lost so much.

Unless that was the wrong way to understand the situation. I tried to keep my tone light.

"If I tempt you with bad things—like this—that's something you could report to her, right?" And seeing the hurt in his face, and knowing the feeling, I said swiftly, "That's what we're being set up for, isn't it? Unless it's not. Unless Captain Lotuk is throwing us together for some other reason."

Ateni's face closed and he shook his head. But I pressed on.

"I know you think Civil Order—and the academy and, well, the whole Polity—is against you, but if she wanted to, Captain Lotuk could have stuck by her original charges against you, claimed a bombing was responsible for the damage to Daybreak Ventures, and you'd be facing a half-decade of reeducation in confinement instead of being finished after two months," I insisted. "But she didn't do that. Why not? And if you and I are such a potentially dangerous combination, why push us together? I think she's decided we're *not* a danger and wants something else from us."

"And you want to give it to her?" There was something in his tone that reminded me of his foster brother.

"No!" I said, "I don't care what she wants. What she wants isn't important. It's what *we* want—what we want her to understand and recognize."

The last ragged bit of poinsettia leaf was still in Ateni's hand. He turned it over, turned it over again.

"She's just one person. If she falls into heterodoxy, Civil Order will just turn on her," he said. But now he was looking at me like he wanted to be persuaded.

"I don't think we have to think that far ahead. I just want you to keep on teaching ancient history and historical excavation, and if you can't do it officially—well, Captain Lotuk is someone who's literally demanding to read your thoughts. And meanwhile, maybe we'll be turning up other students-who-don't-know-they're-students." As I said it, Tailin sprang to mind, unenthusiastic though he'd been about the Mudhugger thesis.

Ateni looked at me aslant, smiling. "You know, Paru has you all wrong," he said. "I still think it would be safer to bore the captain to death, but nothing's ever really safe, and I do want to share what I learn." He shrugged, let the last piece of the poinsettia leaf flutter to the ground. "Let's get some juice and hear some of Kadiuk's stories," he said. We linked arms and headed back toward the retired Sweet Harbor gods.

About the Author

Francesca Forrest is the author of *Lagoonfire*'s predecessor story, *The Inconvenient God,* as well as *Pen Pal* (2013), a hard-to-classify novel from the margins. Her short stories have appeared in *Not One of Us, Strange Horizons, Fireside Fiction,* and other online and print venues. She's currently working on a third story about Decommissioner Thirty-Seven that builds on the events in *Lagoonfire.*

She blogs at asakiyume.dreamwidth.org, and you can follow her on Twitter at @morinotsuma.

About the Publisher

Annorlunda Books is a small press that publishes books to inform, entertain, and make you think. We publish short books (novella length or shorter) and collections of short writing, fiction and non-fiction.

Find more information about us and our books online: annorlundaenterprises.com/books or follow us on Twitter: @AnnorlundaInc.

To stay up to date on all of our releases, subscribe to our mailing list at:

annorlundaenterprises.com/mailing-list

Selected Other Titles from Annorlunda Books

Short Books

The Inconvenient God, by Francesca Forrest, is a fantasy novelette about a government official tasked with retiring a god who isn't quite ready to leave.

The Lilies of Dawn, by Vanessa Fogg, is a fantasy novelette about a young woman who must summon all of her courage and strength to face a threat to the lilies on which her village depends.

The Boy Who was Mistaken for a Fairy King, by HL Fullerton, is a novella about an average boy... who sometimes confers with trees and just happens to have antlers growing on his head, and an average girl who is enthralled with the chase, and what happens when someone calls a Hunt.

Water into Wine, by Joyce Chng, a sci-fi novella about a family trying to build a life amidst an interstellar war that threatens everything.

Tattoo, by Michelle Rene, a novella about a young woman who appears in a cynical post-Judgement Day age, and the band of strangers who find themselves called to keep her safe.

Okay, So Look and *Here's the Deal* by Micah Edwards, are humorous, yet accurate and thought-provoking, retellings of the Book of Genesis and the Book of Exodus.

Arctic Adagio, by DJ Cockburn, a mystery novelette set in an all-too-believable near future in which the super rich have bought their way free of the law.

The Dodo King, by Michelle Rene, is a novella that tells the story of the friendship between Louis Carrol and Alice Liddell, his muse for *Alice in Wonderland*, through Alice's eyes.

Unspotted, by Justin Fox, is the story of the Cape Mountain Leopard and the author's own journey to try to see one.

The Burning, by J.P. Seewald, a novella set in the coal country of Pennsylvania, about a family struggling to cope as a slow-moving catastrophe threatens everything they have.

Caresaway, by DJ Cockburn, a near future "inside your head" thriller about a scientist who discovers a cure for depression, but finds that it comes at a terrible cost.

Don't Call It Bollywood, by Margaret E. Redlich, is an introduction to the world of Hindi film.

Collections

Both Sides of My Skin, by Elizabeth Trach, a collection of short stories exploring the reality of pregnancy and motherhood.

Nontraditional, by Nan Kuhlman, a collection of linked essays about teaching in a community college. Kuhlman introduces us to her students, the lessons she taught... and the lessons she learned along the way

Hemmed In, a Taster Flight collection of classic short stories about women's lives.

Love and Other Happy Endings is a Taster Flight collection of classic stories, all of which end on a high note.

Missed Chances is another Taster Flight of classic stories about love and "the one that got away."

Small and Spooky is a Taster Flight of classic ghost stories, all of which feature a child.

Academaze, by Sydney Phlox, is a collection of essays and cartoons about life in academia.

CPSIA information can be obtained
at www.ICGtesting.com
Printed in the USA
LVHW090959190221
679462LV00005B/1112